Agent Svetlana Simonov of the government's top-secret Omega Force is sent to Florida to find out if a former secret agent killed his family, then himself, or if something more sinister has happened. In Florida she comes across the beautiful Katrina Luvesky, leader of the deadly Moscow Cartel. Svetlana must infiltrate Katrina's network and stop it before the United States finds itself in an international drug war. Passion and violence erupt as Svetlana and Katrina do battle.

This book is a work of fiction. Names, characters, places, and incidents either are products of the author's imagination or are used fictitiously. Any resemblance to actual events or locales or persons, living or dead, is entirely coincidental.

Deadly Secrets
Copyright © 2020 Robin Gideon
ISBN: 978-1-4874-2874-7
Cover art by Martine Jardin

Published by eXtasy Books Inc or
Devine Destinies, an imprint of eXtasy Books Inc

Look for us online at:
www.eXtasybooks.com or www.devinedestinies.com

DEADLY SECRETS
AGENT (ROM)ANTICS BOOK 2

BY

ROBIN GIDEON

DEDICATION

This one is for my bff CFL, who knows how to keep secrets.

CHAPTER ONE

Florida Keys, United States

Katrina Luvesky looked at the four young mercenaries and wondered if they were as willing to kill unarmed men, women, and children as she believed. The four men looked fit enough for the task, all of them tall and thick-chested, with that slightly under-fed look that carnivorous animals possessed when they hadn't made a kill in a while and an empty stomach gnawed at them.

"Tonight, we will begin a new phase of our operation, and you will be at the forefront of that mission," she said, keeping her voice low so that the men were forced to concentrate to hear everything she said. "Tonight, the Moscow Cartel, the most powerful criminal organization the world has ever known, takes root in the United States."

Katrina paused a moment, turning away from the men to look at Juanita Diego. The young petite Mexican girl was standing impassively, her dark eyes seeing everything while showing no emotion. She was Katrina's closest assistant, and she followed orders without hesitation or question.

Physically, Katrina was in stark contrast to her. The Russian was tall, standing an even six feet in height, and her eyes were the color of blue ice. Katrina's breasts were full and round. She was, overall, spectacularly feminine, and as deadly a creature as had ever walked the Earth.

"We need everyone inside the residence neutralized," Katrina continued, speaking to the four soldiers, though she was looking at Juanita. "There can be no one left alive. Later, when the property is put up for sale, the Moscow Cartel will purchase the land, using a front to avoid whatever complications the American legal system puts forward."

Katrina stepped closer to a soldier. His name was Jacques. He was the most attractive of the four soldiers, and like the others, in his early twenties. He was muscular and handsome and heartless, which, for Katrina, made him close to perfect for her needs. She wondered just how endowed he was. No doubt he would not compare to Katrina's favorite, the hulking mute Russian named Vladimir—who had the richly deserved nickname of "Vlad the Impaler."

"Juanita, come closer," Katrina said quietly, looking at Jacques's handsome profile.

The four young soldiers stood at attention, their arms at their sides, chests out and shoulders square. Each man wore a drab olive green and brown camouflaged military uniform. Katrina touched Jacques's chest with a fingertip as though testing the firmness of fruit in a grocery store. The young man continued staring straight ahead.

"Juanita, I want you to sharpen their senses," Katrina continued.

Katrina let her finger run down Jacques's chest, then over his flat stomach. He continued staring straight ahead, just as he had been trained to. Katrina felt a tingling begin inside herself, a delightful itching sensation centered down low, in her clitoris. Katrina reached between Jacques's legs. She squeezed his cock through the camouflaged trousers, and was pleased with what she felt. As she fondled him, his cock almost immediately began growing longer and harder. That, too, pleased Katrina. Immensely.

Juanita, with her midnight black hair falling over her shoulders nearly to her trim waist, stood quietly, waiting for the next order to be given.

"Yes, you are definitely all man, aren't you?" It was really more of a statement of fact than a question.

Jacques did not reply. He did not turn his gaze directly toward her, even though his cock was rapidly hardening, creating a prominent bulge in his uniform.

Katrina caught the tab of his fly zipper and tugged it down. She reached inside Jacques's uniform, and her fingers curled gently around the growing shaft of his cock. She felt the heat of his strong young body go through her palm, into her blood. His heart accelerated and quickly made his cock fill her fist.

"Very nice," Katrina purred. It took a bit of doing, but she finally got his cock out of his trousers. His long, pale column of hard flesh filled her hand. "Juanita, give him some pleasure, but not too much. He mustn't be satisfied, just pleasured. Do you understand?"

"Yes, Comrade Luvesky," Juanita replied dutifully.

Without hesitation, Juanita moved so that she stood directly in front of Jacques. She was barely five feet tall, and the soldier towered over her. Slowly, drawing out the suspense of the moment, Juanita sank to her knees. She smoothed her hair behind her ears, and for several seconds remained motionless, her hands resting lightly on her thighs. Her onyx-black eyes took on a new brilliance as she watched Katrina's hand moving back and forth over the pulsing shaft of Jacques's cock.

"Go ahead, Juanita," Katrina whispered huskily. "Give him some pleasure."

The pink tip of Juanita's tongue made a slow circumference of her mouth, moistening her lips. Then she leaned forward and kissed the flaring crown of Jacques's cock. Her tongue slithered out between her lips. The soft, sultry purr of contentment that came from Juanita was unaffected. Her dark eyes were open, but they had taken on a smoky quality, as though the young woman was slowly sinking into a trance. After several seconds, she pushed forward, filling her mouth with the soldier's cock. Her jaws opened wide. She tightened her lips around the thick, heavily veined shaft, just behind the head of his cock. Her tongue was in constant motion.

"Is she good?" Katrina asked Jacques. She knew of Juanita's skill in such matters. He continued staring straight ahead. Katrina simply smiled and, as she worked her hand back and forth over his shaft, she let her fingers occasionally brush against Juanita's mouth. "Yes, my darling Juanita can give great pleasure. There are times, at the end of a long and difficult day, when the pressures of being a senior officer for the Moscow Cartel can seem overwhelming. Juanita helps me relax. She likes helping me relax. Don't you, Juanita?"

Juanita let Jacques slide out of her mouth. Looking up at Katrina, with the moist tip of Jacques's cock brushing her chin, she answered, "Yes, Comrade Luvesky. I like helping you relax. It is my job to do whatever you ask of me."

"Good girl," Katrina replied. She guided the cock to Juanita's lips. "Now continue with your comrade. Make his senses razor-sharp, but you mustn't satisfy him. If he's satisfied, then I will be displeased—" her tone dipped menacingly—"and then I would need to punish you."

Katrina knew that Juanita both adored and feared her. For Juanita, Katrina was not simply her superior within the paramilitary criminal organization known as the Moscow Cartel, she was her master. When the Iron Curtain fell and the walls came crumbling down, organized crime flourished in the power vacuum. Katrina grew up understanding she was one of the people to see the potential for profits. Years later, when she took Juanita as a personal aide within the organization, it was a life-altering day for the girl.

"Very good," Katrina purred, drawling the first word out slowly, lewdly. "I have obviously taught you well. Yes, Juanita . . . you've always been a good student. One of the best

I've ever had."

Katrina looked at the soldier's face. It seemed like his features had been chiseled from granite. It was only by peering into the young man's eyes that Katrina could tell he was straining desperately to keep the pleasure that surged through his body from showing in his expression. Katrina smiled, pleased with the young man's discipline. He was exactly the kind of well-trained young killer that the Moscow Cartel needed if it was to become the most powerful and most secretive criminal organization in the world.

How much more pleasure could the young man withstand, Katrina wondered idly as she studied his harsh but handsome face. She decided that he'd had enough. If he released his passion, then his reflexes would lose their critical edge. That was something that Katrina simply couldn't allow.

"That's enough," she said sharply to Juanita. "Over here now. There's more that need your attention."

Juanita abandoned Jacques without so much as a sideways glance. She crawled on her hands and knees until she was in front of Arturo.

"Not him," Katrina barked. "Over here. In front of Petyr, so that you can give all three of them pleasure!"

Juanita did precisely as she had been ordered, her tiny hands and warm, soft lips simultaneously exciting three soldiers to a fever-pitch, taking them to the edge of the abyss without letting them release their passion.

"That's good," Katrina purred, looking down at her protégé's performance as the young woman bobbed slowly back and forth, alternately sucking on three cocks. "Your studies are progressing wonderfully. Excite, but do not satisfy. That reward is for later, after they have successfully completed the mission Mr. Bigg has for him."

Katrina took a step backward so that she had a more complete view of Juanita and the men. These were the hand-picked unit she had selected for the Moscow Cartel's American operation. Each person had been trained and cross-trained. She watched as Juanita performed, giving the blow-jobs in a manner that was to be seen as well as felt, and the temperature gauge in Katrina's blood inched upward. She suddenly found herself envious of Juanita's petite physique, of her youth, of the waist-length black hair that shimmered in the sunlight like liquid ink.

In a stern tone, Katrina commanded the girl, "Take him deeper."

Juanita made a valiant effort, but her body resisted, despite her ardent struggle. She coughed and sputtered on the cock that filled her mouth and threatened to enter her throat.

After several seconds of strain, Katrina said quietly, with just the right amount of maternal disapproval and love, "That's quite enough. Let me show you how it's to be done."

Katrina got down on her knees beside Juanita. The ebony-haired beauty released the soldier from her oral embrace. Katrina opened her mouth and swallowed the soldier's cock in a single, smooth motion, not stopping until her nose was pressed against the brass teeth of Petyr's zipper. His hard erection visibly swelled her neck. Embracing in her mouth and throat every hard inch of cock the soldier possessed, Katrina purred softly, knowing she was not simply giving the soldier pleasure, she was also impressing the soldiers and Juanita with her sexual supremacy. Seconds ticked by slowly. Katrina reached around the young soldier's trim hips and cupped his taut buns, holding him tightly, his throbbing cock buried in her throat. When Katrina finally leaned back, her lips gliding along the cock's shaft as his hard flesh slipped out of her throat, she was vividly aware of Juanita's dark, envious gaze upon her. She kissed the knob of the soldier's cock and resisted the urge to smile.

"That's how it's done," she said with a stern, authoritarian tone in her voice.

The surface of Katrina's skin was tingling, as though she was receiving low-voltage electrical current. She wondered how many of the four soldiers she would have for her own pleasure once the mission was accomplished. She usually didn't have sex with low-ranking soldiers, though sometimes it was an erotic way to spend a few idle hours. Mostly, Katrina saved her passion for the amazingly endowed Russian nick-named Vlad the Impaler. And Juanita, of course.

"That's enough," Katrina said, when she decided the soldiers had received enough pleasure to sharpen their senses to a dangerous, lethal edge. "You men will be rewarded after you have successfully completed your mission."

The mansion in the cove was surrounded by an eight-foot-high white marble wall. The original owner had been a member of the New York Mafia, and he'd been more than merely paranoid for his safety, since he had ordered the murders of enough of his former associates, enemies, and friends, to have an on-going "contract" on his head.

As it turned out, the mobster had been safe and protected within the marble walls of his Florida Keys retreat. But his taste for Chinese cuisine was his undoing. He'd been hunched over a heaping plate of sub gum chow mien in a tiny Chinese restaurant when a lone gunman put a .45 automatic to the back of the mob kingpin's head and pulled the trigger.

The current owner of the residence—which included a main house with five bathrooms, five bedrooms, a ballroom large enough to accommodate a party of one hundred comfortably, and three separate fireplaces that had been converted to gas within the past decade—enjoyed the privacy the marble wall gave him more than the protection.

He should have been more concerned with his protection.

Four men and one slender woman, all wearing camouflaged uniforms, slipped quietly over the marble wall. Each
soldier was equipped with a Colt Police Positive .38 Special,
fitted with a silencer and loaded with hollow-point bullets
that had been made into *dum-dums* by having an X filed into
each one. Upon impact the bullets didn't merely mushroom,
they splintered into small segments. The woman did not carry
a pistol. Instead, she had in her back pocket a black-handled
stiletto-bladed switchblade. It was her weapon of choice. She
preferred her killing to be done up close and with a personal
touch.

The secluded mansion's owner was an English gentleman
named Sir Malcomb Sitwell. His family — a wife and two
sons — owned three cats but no dogs. The cats, upon discovering the intruders, quietly crept to safe shadows, concerned
only with their own welfare as the Sitwells slept.

The maid, an elderly immigrant from Germany who often
had trouble sleeping throughout the night, had taken two
sleeping pills at midnight, afraid that her chronic insomnia
would afflict her. She was dreaming of her childhood home
in Munich when Jacques entered her bedroom. The room was
far removed from the other bedrooms, separated not because
of her social status compared to the Sitwells, but because of
the volume at which she snored.

Jacques paused a moment to look at the old woman. He
waited a second. No more than that. He aimed his Police Positive at her forehead and squeezed the trigger. The long silencer reduced the pistol's roar to a hiss. The hollow-point
dum-dum, upon striking the maid's skull, fragmented into
four separate pieces of lead and copper. The old woman's
head literally exploded.

In other rooms in the mansion, victims were dispatched in
similar fashion. Neither of Sir Malcomb's sons heard a thing
as they were executed while sleeping.

Sir Malcomb had retired while in his late forties from the British military. He had bravely served his twenty years, and when he met a wealthy American widow, he moved from London to Florida without remorse. Peace, love, and family contentment had dulled what had for many years been battle-honed senses.

Jacques, Arturo, Deiter, and Petyr were all in the bedroom when Sir Malcomb was shaken awake, a large gloved hand over his mouth to prevent him from making even a sound. Jacques looked into Sir Malcomb's eyes and put a gloved finger to his own lips, indicating silence. Then Sir Malcomb was assisted out of the bed while his wife slept peacefully.

In the library, Juanita extracted from a canvas pouch a bottle of vodka. It was one hundred proof. She opened the bottle, breaking the seal, and pointed toward the overstuffed chair near the fireplace.

"What's the meaning of this?" Sir Malcomb asked, finally finding his voice.

The uniformed soldiers said nothing. Juanita extended the vodka bottle.

"Take this. Drink."

"No."

"Drink it," Juanita said quietly. "If you don't, we'll kill your wife."

The defiance drained quickly out of Sir Malcomb. His gaze darted left and right. .

"What are you worried about?" Juanita asked. "If we wanted you dead, your brains would be on the floor. Now take the bottle and drink. Finish it all and nothing will happen to you. I promise."

Malcomb took the bottle and brought it to his lips. It took him almost five minutes to drink the entire pint of liquor.

Deiter stepped into the library. He nodded his head, saying nothing. When he did, the faintest smile curled Juanita's lips.

"Very good," she said. She placed the bottle on the carpeted floor beside Malcomb. "Just sit there now. Everything will be just fine in a matter of minutes."

Juanita watched as the alcohol began clouding Malcomb's brain. She saw him blinking his eyes as he tried to clear his vision. It was a pleasure to watch the capitalist trying to intellectualize his way past the alcohol that was fogging and diluting his reasoning. Three times Juanita walked past him, moving just a little closer each time. He stopped watching her carefully.

Juanita brought out a second bottle. She opened the vodka, breaking the seal. This time she did not hand the bottle to Sir Malcomb. Rather, she put it to his lips and forced his head back. He clearly knew what was expected, and gulped the clear, fiery liquid as best he could. Vodka dribbled over his chin and down his neck, only to get soaked up in his fine silk pajamas.

"That should do it," Juanita said when the last of the second bottle of vodka had, quite literally, been poured down Sir Malcomb's throat.

She waited until she was on the verge of losing consciousness before she took the .38 Special from Deiter. She unscrewed the silencer and then placed the weapon in Sir Malcomb's relaxed hand. He said something, or at least tried to say something. Saliva trickled from the corner of his mouth.

Juanita turned the weapon inside Malcomb's hand so that the muzzle touched his temple. He started to protest, fighting against the young Mexican woman with the fathomless black eyes.

The Colt Police Positive roared, the deafening noise of the .38 Special being fired echoing off the walls. The force of the fragmenting round bursting through hard skull and soft brain tissue tossed Sir Malcomb out of the chair. The left side of his head had disintegrated.

CHAPTER TWO

Washington D.C.

"It doesn't add up," Jefferson Burke said, sitting at a desk in Svetlana Simonov's luxury hotel room. She sat in a chair facing him. He was her controller at the government's ultra-secret Omega Force. "He wasn't the kind of man to do such a thing."

"Psyches break," Svetlana replied. "It's unfortunate, but it happens, sir."

She had just finished reading the journalism account on an e-reader of how Sir Malcolm Sitwell had, apparently in a drunken stupor, shot and killed his wife, two sons, and maid. Then he turned the weapon on himself. It appeared to be a pretty clear-cut case of murder/suicide.

"I knew Malcolm Sitwell, and he wouldn't snap. Not like that. He adored his wife and children." Burke ran fingers through his thick black hair that was prematurely graying at the temples. "Malcolm and I had been friends for a long time. We'd been on half a dozen joint British/American assignments together, so I'm telling you that I knew the man. He might kill himself, but he certainly wouldn't murder his family. And there are other inconsistencies."

"Such as?"

"It seems there were a number of people who heard a single gunshot that night, but nobody recalls hearing *more* than the single shot."

"Yes, that is curious, isn't it," Svetlana replied. She crossed her legs at the knee, felt the slide of silk stocking against silk, and felt her most intimate place tingling slightly. Svetlana sensed a new mission would soon be assigned, and that was making her senses fine-tuned. She tried to remember her last satisfying sexual encounter, then pushed the thought away. For now.

"Are you having trouble concentrating, Svetlana?" Burke asked sharply.

"No!" Svetlana's reply was quick, a bit defensive. She forced all thoughts of sexual entanglements out of her mind, and looked straight into Burke's eyes. "I was just wondering what exactly it is you're asking me to do."

Burke looked away. Svetlana sensed there was a personal element to this assignment that he was uncomfortable with. She suspected it was strictly against policy at Omega Force to allow personal feelings to affect decisions. She didn't know much about the shadowy organization called Omega Force, which she worked for, but she knew that much.

"Frankly, even I'm not certain what I'm asking you to do," Burke explained, his voice low, unusually soft. "I guess I just want you to go to Florida and look around a bit. Find out what you can. If it's true that Malcolm went off the deep end and murdered his family and then killed himself, then I'll have to accept that. But I need to be convinced that's what he did."

"You think the Florida police might have botched up the investigation?"

"They might have botched it up, or maybe they just wanted an easy answer." He looked at Svetlana, his eyes filled with sincerity. "You're a top agent, Svetlana. I think the best ever to have worked for me. I trust your judgment. Go to Florida and look around. Find out what you can. If Malcolm committed suicide, don't spare me the ugly truth."

"And if he didn't commit suicide?"

"Then find out what happened and who is responsible.

You have complete authority to take this investigation wher-ever it leads."

Svetlana got to her feet.

"I'll get right on it, sir."

"You've got a flight booked for thirteen hundred hours," Burke said. "Be careful, Svetlana. There's something about this that isn't what it seems."

"Careful? Always."

CHAPTER THREE

"Good. Very good. But there's still something we haven't addressed."

Svetlana felt her heart skip several beats. Burke's tone of voice had changed, becoming low, ominous but yet supremely exciting. She'd been working for Omega Force for ten years, which meant she'd had her assignments directed by Jefferson Burke for ten years. He was the only person in Omega Force she'd ever truly known, and for years now the only one she ever saw. She took her orders from him, and him alone.

And she followed every order that he gave her. Every one. Without exception or even delay.

"Yes," Svetlana said, looking down at the floor, her voice a whisper. "I know that, sir."

"Your last assignment was successful, was it not?"

"Yes, sir."

"You were assigned to eliminate a bomb maker who has worked against the United States. You eliminated him, didn't you? In fact, you did that by using one of his own bombs against him." Svetlana looked up just in time to see him give a lopsided, rather cruel smile. "I like the irony of that." He stepped closer, and Svetlana once against felt her heart stutter. "But more than just killing a bomb maker, you did something else to him, didn't you?"

Svetlana tried to speak, discovered her mouth was too dry for words, then gave her head the briefest nod. Her hair moved against her shoulders and down her back. For several seconds she let the tip of her tongue make a quick, furtive circumstance of her lips.

Burke stepped even closer, raised his right hand, and touched the tip of his forefinger to the underside of her chin, then raised her face sufficiently for him to look directly into her eyes. "You got down on your knees for him, didn't you?"

"It was to gain his trust," she said, closing her eyes briefly before opening them again. "I never meant anything romantic or even sexual about it. I only did it so that he'd let his guard down, so that he'd trust me more." She closed her eyes briefly. "He was very suspicious of me. He was suspicious of everyone."

"So you gave him a blow job." It was a statement, not a question.

"I needed to get inside his compound. I needed him to take me there, or else I'd never have gotten through his security. So I did what I had to do to complete the mission."

Svetlana watched as Burke's gaze went downward, then lingered on her breasts. She knew her blouse showed some cleavage, but not an ostentatious or indecent amount. Svetlana felt her nipples get just a little tighter, a little more pebbled. She could feel her clit throbbing, and the lips of her pussy become moist. This was the effect Burke always had on her.

"Yes, you only did what you had to do. Or so you say. But as your commanding officer, I have a duty to punish you for bad behavior . . . don't I?"

Svetlana uttered a short, soft gasp and felt her lips move as though she was speaking, though no sound came out. After several seconds of weighty silence, she nodded.

"Your punishment shouldn't hurt . . . too much," Burke said. He cupped Svetlana's face between his palms and rubbed the pad of one thumb back and forth over her lips. "You'll only get what's coming to you. Only what you deserve."

Slowly and deliberately, Burke began unbuttoning Svetlana's silk blouse. His fingers were deft and made quick work of the buttons. When he reached the buckle of her belt, he tugged the blouse tails out of her waistband and finished the job. Very slowly, as though unwrapping an infinitely precious gift, he opened her blouse to expose her breasts. She hoped he appreciated the white, lace-trimmed and hand-tailored brassiere she'd selected that morning.

He walked behind Svetlana and slowly slid her blouse over her shoulders, then down her arms. His palms skimmed lightly over her skin. When the blouse was tugged past her hands, Burke cast it casually on the nearby king-size hotel bed. Still standing where she couldn't see him, Svetlana felt the clasp of her bra between her shoulder blades get unfastened, and the cups loosened their hold on her breasts.

Svetlana felt her cunt tighten and fresh nectar make her entrance dewy, ready for penetration.

He reached around her body with his hands, unbuckled her belt, then pulled it slowly through the loops until it was completely free of her skirt. What did he plan with that belt?

Her senses were so fine-tuned that she could hear the brass teeth of the skirt's zipper at the small of her back releasing, one by one.

Burke's really taking his time, drawing this out. This might be an all-nighter!

He eased her skirt over the sweeping curve of her hips, and it slithered down to pool around her ankles. When Burke got down on one knee and touched her ankle, Svetlana stepped out of the skirt without getting out of her stilettos. She was now wearing only her shoes and thong panties. She kept her hands at her sides, and could almost feel the heat of Burke's body. He was close enough that she could smell his masculine Old Spice aftershave. Every nerve ending in Svetlana was crackling with electrical, sexual tension. She felt herself on the brink of a climax, even though she hadn't actually been caressed.

"Put your hands behind your back," Burke said. Svetlana caught her lower lip between her teeth and bit briefly. "Cross them at the wrists." She didn't move, but her heart was hammering in her chest. "If you delay, it'll only make your punishment that much worse."

She followed the orders that had been given to her, and a moment later her own Italian leather belt was wrapped several times around her bare wrists, then buckled properly. Svetlana's breathing, now that she was in bondage, came faster and more deeply. She breathed through her mouth, not her nose. The intensity of the situation was escalating rapidly.

Burke walked around until he was in front of Svetlana. Despite herself, Svetlana's gaze dipped from his face to his crotch. The long prominent bulge of an erection trapped inside his hand-tailored trousers was impressive in length and girth, and Svetlana's libido responded accordingly. Though she didn't want to admit to herself and never would to anyone else, in her libido, size mattered. A lot.

Thank God Burke's hung like a horse and virile as a stallion.

"Oh God," Svetlana whispered, and for several seconds she couldn't turn her gaze away from the masculine bounty that Burke represented. He was a feast, a banquet, a smorgasbord. Her thong was white, matching her bra, and she hoped that a wet spot wasn't visible. Burke had set the stage very nicely for an hours-long command performance.

Burke eased his right hand inside the waistband of Svetlana's panties, touching her flesh with the backs of his fingers. He looked straight into her eyes, his face now so close to Svetlana that she could feel his breath, and smell the pleasing, manly scent of his after shave.

"Pretty panties," he said, the timbre of his voice deep, sensually masculine. "They're very tiny . . . but they're in my way."

In the next instant, his right hand clenched into a fist, and then he pulled away sharply. Svetlana's hips were thrust forward, and she felt the panties bite into the tender flesh of her hips, then heard the damning rip of sheer cotton giving way to much greater strength.

The eroticism of having Burke bind her hands behind her back, then rip off her panties, was nearly enough to make her climax then and there. She was teetering on the brink even though she hadn't truly been intimately caressed.

Burke had that effect on her.

Svetlana tested the belt surrounding her wrists and found that there was no give, no yield. Her own Donna Karon belt would be around her wrists until Burke himself took it off. She was in bondage and helpless until Burke decided to set her free.

Svetlana was hoping that freedom wouldn't come anytime soon. Her cunt was creaming, and she ached for sexual release.

Burke put his hand, palm upward, between her slightly spread, naked thighs.

"Oh, God!" Svetlana gasped, and her knees partially buckled beneath her.

Right from the very beginning of their relationship, Burke's touch had always been electrifying, but on this occasion, it seemed to be particularly high voltage. A single fingertip slipped between the lips of her pussy, pushing in an inch, but not much more than that. Svetlana could hardly breathe.

"I'm . . . so close. So close already." She spoke the final word with a awe in her tone. Burke could often bring her to climax quickly—he was the only man whose sensual arts were skillful enough to cause an orgasm in Svetlana—but even for him, this was almost frighteningly fast.

Svetlana suspected that her on-rushing climax was more caused by the erotic foreplay he'd done with her mind than it

was with the caresses he'd given her body. Svetlana wondered if Burke could make her come just from talking to her
in that naughty way of his that made her want to be ravished
by him with every ounce of strength and virility he possessed.

Burke took his hand away from Svetlana, then shrugged
out of his hand-tailored suit coat and tossed it onto the bed.
With deliberate indolence, he unbuckled his belt, unfastened
the waistband button, then very slowly tugged down the zipper.

Svetlana tried to keep her gaze on his face, but she couldn't.
She looked down, and when Burke exposed his spectacularly
formed erection, a soft gasp caught in her throat, and she felt
her clit throb with wanton excitement. The warm fluids of her
passion moistened the lips of her cunt, preparing her for penetration. Her mouth watered like a starving woman catching
the scent of a steak being expertly cooked on a charcoal grill.

"You've behaved badly." The statement came from Burke
with the warmth of an iceberg. "When women repent,
shouldn't they be on their knees?"

Svetlana nodded, then silently sank to her knees on the
thick carpet in front of Burke. She was distinctly and erotically
aware of the fact that her hands were bound behind her back.
She ignore the tingling in her clit.

Svetlana looked directly at Burke's cock. *Fuck – that's big.*

She wasn't a woman easily impressed in sexual matters.

Burke impressed her in a thousand different ways. And so
did his cock, independent of everything else about him. Especially when it was rock-solid hard and looked as delicious as
anything she'd ever imagined.

Burke reached down and combed his fingers through Svetlana's hair, destroying her carefully constructed coiffeur. He
looked down into her eyes.

"Suck," he said.

There was no ambiguity in the single word. Svetlana

would suck his cock until he decided she should stop. Svetlana's will wasn't part of the equation. This awareness made Svetlana's cunt just a little bit more creamy. She was his willing submissive, and she accepted that role with multi-orgasmic delight.

"But—" she said.

Though there might have been more words she had intended to speak, they were silenced when Burke pushed the head of his cock against her lips, and a moment later, thrust into her mouth until the crown of his erection was pressing tightly against the back of her mouth and threatening to enter her throat. He held his cockhead there, at her throat's entrance, as Svetlana squirmed on her knees, fighting to keep from gagging.

Fuck. Svetlana struggled against the belt that bound her wrists, erotically enjoying the feel of the supple leather, even though she knew she shouldn't. *This time he's going to pull out all the stops. This time he really is going to punish me.*

Suddenly he pulled completely out of her mouth. Svetlana wasn't sure whether she should be relieved or disappointed.

With slow deliberation, Burke walked around Svetlana until he was once again behind her. He grabbed her where the belt was secured and raised her hands, forcing her to bend at the waist. Her breasts swayed away from her body, and Svetlana heard Burke groan, almost as though he was in physical pain.

She watched as Burke, still holding her wrists so that she was bent over, picked up his leather belt that he had dropped ever-so innocently onto the bed some minutes before. He held the buckle in his hand with the opposite end of the belt, so that the leather was doubled in half

Now she suspected it wasn't so innocent.

"When you sucked his cock, did he come in your mouth?" Burke asked as he raised Svetlana's hands just a little higher. She was now bent over sharply at the waist, and her hands were nearly pointing straight toward the ceiling. "And when he fucked you, did he come in your cunt? More importantly, did *you* come?"

Svetlana squeezed her eyes tightly shut. If she told the truth, she would pay a price. If she lied, she'd pay an even more painful price.

Seconds ticked by in total silence. Burke raised her wrists several inches higher, forcing her to bend even more sharply at the waist. Finally, though she couldn't speak, she nodded.

"Bitch," Burke said, and a moment later brought the belt he held in his right hand sharply forward in an arch that brought the two-inch-wide leather into sharp contact with Svetlana's ass.

She cried out when the belt struck her sensitive skin, the leather striking the cheeks with a *crack* that reverberated off the walls of the luxury hotel room.

The sound of the leather hitting her bottom was caused more by the two halves of the leather belt striking each other than by the leather punishing Svetlana's bare flesh. The leather belt was a dog whose bark was much worse than his bite.

Then *crack-crack-crack* in quick succession.

Svetlana cried out every time the belt came down hard on her buns. Each stinging swat of the leather caused her cunt to get just a little bit more juicy, just a little bit more hungry for the sexual fulfillment that only Burke could give her.

"Bitch!" Burke whispered.

He released her wrists. She immediately stood upright, her naked breasts rising and falling with her rapid breathing. Her bottom was tingling, and she wondered if the cheeks of her ass were merely pink, or downright red. Burke had taken her to the brink.

Burke positioned Svetlana so that she stood in front of the office chair he had vacated. His eyes practically glowed with lust. Svetlana wondered if that was how a wolf looked when he was on the hunt, moving in for the kill.

When Burke tossed his belt back onto the bed, Svetlana knew that at least part of her "punishment" was over with. But what was to come next? Burke was a masterful Dom, and he always seemed to come up with something new after Svetlana finished an assignment and had done something that *needed punishment.*

"So beautiful. So deadly."

He cupped her breasts in his hands, lifting them. He squeezed the mounds from the sides, making her nipples become even more pronounced. Very slowly, he bent at the waist, then sucked Svetlana's right nipple between his lips. The heat and moisture of his mouth on her sensitive breast added significantly to Svetlana's passion, and she had to consciously keep her feet beneath her or she would fall to the floor in a swoon.

After a full minute of sucking and licking on her right nipple, Burke turned his attention to her left. Once again, he moved at a leisurely pace, a man in complete control of his world . . . and of everyone in it.

By the time Burke finally straightened his back, Svetlana's nipples were throbbing with sexual tension just as much as her clit. When he caught her nipples between curled forefingers and thumbs, then caressed softly, Svetlana let her head roll back on her shoulders, and she issued a soft, warbling sigh of primal passion.

"So . . . treacherous."

There was something ominous in how Burke had pronounced the last word that made her eyes shoot open wide.

She had just enough time to look at Burke before he pinched her nipples hard enough to make her gasp in pain. She looked into his fathomless eyes, her teeth clenched, her lips pulled back to reveal them.

"You have something to say?" Burke asked in a

conversational tone, as though he wasn't really, at that very moment, administering edge-of-the-envelope tit torture. He pulled upward on her nipples, distorting their shape. "Perhaps you have a complaint you'd like to make?"

Svetlana shook her head. She rose up onto her tiptoes, but since she was already in five-inch heels, she couldn't get much higher to relieve the pressure Burke was administering.

Burke held her like that for long seconds, the natural shape of Svetlana's breasts distorted while they were being raised by her nipples. Just when she was about to cry out her safe word—the word that would tell Burke he had gone too far, that she could take no more, and that he must stop immediately—Burke released his punishing grip. Once freed, Svetlana's breasts resumed their normal shape, and then to her exquisite delight, Burke soothed away her discomfort by licking and sucking tenderly on both nipples for what seemed like an eternity.

He could make me come just from sucking on my nipples. How can any man learn to have sensual skills like that?

He put his hand on Svetlana's shoulder, then gave her a shove that sent to tumbling into the padded chair at the desk. Sitting, her mouth was at cock-level to Burke, and though she knew she shouldn't smile, her lips curled upward at the corners. If he wanted to fuck her mouth, he could. Svetlana had neither the ability nor the inclination to stop him.

Burke sank to the floor between Svetlana's wide-spread thighs

He's going to fuck me. Finally! She looked down through the valley of her quivering breasts as Burke rubbed the saliva-moistened conical head of his cock up and down over the lips of her pussy. He did it slowly, repeatedly, and just when Svetlana was about to beg him for penetration, she watched and felt as the knob of his cock separated the lips of her cunt and began a long, slow invasion.

It took four revolutions of his hips before Burke had

achieved full insertion. When he was completely buried inside her and his body was pressing against her clit, Svetlana arched her back and began to climax.

"Ahhh!" she cried out, her body bucking in the padded chair, her breasts quivering, her thighs clenched around Burke's torso.

The contractions were powerful and numerous. In their years together, Burke had made her climax many, many times, but she could never remember one being this forceful, this all-consuming.

Then Burke grabbed her by the ankles and lifted them until the backs of her calves were up on his broad, naked shoulders. When her head banged against the backrest of the chair, she looked up into his face and saw the fiery glow of an Alpha male who was about to claim his sub.

The pounding that Svetlana received was intense, unchecked in its forcefulness. Again and again Burke drove his hips forward with machine-like fury, his cock tugging and pushing at the lips of Svetlana's entrance, his torso slapping against the backs of her thighs. Svetlana climaxed a second time, and then a third, before Burke let out a lion's roar of triumph and his semen poured from him and into Svetlana in a torrent.

"One more?" The voice was husky, richly masculine, hinting at unimaginable pleasures.

Svetlana's eyes were closed. His breath was warm against her pussy. She was twirling a lock of Burke's hair around the tip of her right forefinger as she basked in the afterglow of multiple orgasms. The first three had happened while Burke had her tied up and sitting in the desk chair. That was when they were playing their D/s game, and the sex was full-on slam fucking. The next happened on the bed, when the belt was no longer around her wrists. They made love slowly and leisurely, tenderly and with great emotion. The last three were when she was spread-eagled on the bed, and Burke's fingers, lips and tongue, were working their magic on nerve endings that were now hypersensitive.

"One more?" he asked again.

"Would I be greedy if I said *yes?*"

She heard him chuckle softly. "Let's just say that you'd be the woman I know you are."

Then she felt him gently close his lips around her clit and slide a finger into her to caress the slick front wall of her cunt, where her g-spot was and she was particularly sensitive.

"Just one more," Svetlana said, knowing with experience that Burke would satisfy her wish and desire.

He always did.

CHAPTER FOUR

Florida Keys, United States

Katrina Luvesky kicked her feet over the edge of the bed and sat up. She was wide awake almost instantly. She looked at the small electric clock on the bedside stand. It was six o'clock in the morning. She smiled, looking around her bedroom. A month earlier, in this same room, Mr. and Mrs. Malcolm Sitwell had slept peacefully. Then her soldiers had entered their bedroom.

Katrina's smile broadened. Her plan had worked perfectly. The investigation into the murder/suicide had been quick, and no one doubted that Malcolm Sitwell, an Englishman living in Florida, had murdered his entire family — including his elderly maid — then committed suicide, apparently in a drunken rage.

All of Katrina's plans of late had worked to perfection. Barely five years earlier, her lover, Alexandr Biggisov, known to friends and enemies as Mr. Bigg, had created the Moscow Cartel. When he died of a heart attack, his body on top of Katrina's as they made passionate love, she had wisely disposed of the corpse herself. She kept the news of his death to herself, too.

At first she hesitantly gave orders to Mr. Bigg's top lieutenants in the Moscow Cartel, telling them that the orders came from Mr. Bigg himself. When the orders were followed without question — everyone knew that Katrina was Mr. Bigg's lover and closest confidante — she realized that the fear of immediate execution for not following one of Mr. Bigg's orders was so intense that nobody dared question whether Katrina was acting on her own, or on Mr. Bigg's behalf.

Mr. Bigg had taught Katrina well, but she had dreams that were even grander than his. This Florida Keys operation was just one part of that grandiose scheme.

Still wearing her floor-length silk nightgown, Katrina got out of bed and stretched her arms over her head. Idly, she wondered if she would have one of her soldiers that day. It was entertaining to have one or more of them to start the day. It always made her thoughts a little clearer whenever she started the morning with a good orgasm. But thoughts of hot sex didn't last long in Katrina's mind. This was an important day, with too much to do and not enough time to fit in personal pleasures.

When she stepped into the kitchen, Jacques was sitting at the kitchen table. He leaped to his feet, snapping to attention. Vlad the Impaler was there, too, and when he jumped to his feet, Katrina could feel the floor shake beneath her high-heeled slippers.

Vlad was truly amazing.

He stood seven feet tall, and weighed over three hundred pounds. His body was so powerful he had the ability to make Katrina, who was six feet tall, feel small and petite. To top it all off, his cock was enormous, the largest one Katrina had ever seen in her life. He was virile, too. He got hard and stayed hard, and when he erupted, he let loose with a flood-tide of semen.

"Is everything going according to plan?" Katrina asked in a no-nonsense tone.

Vlad the Impaler nodded a mute affirmative, continuing to stare straight ahead.

"Good. I will inspect the operation in one hour's time."

She paused a moment to look at Vlad. Katrina always felt

a little more confident whenever he was near. Not only was he the most spectacular stud she'd ever met, he was also the most cold-blooded killer she had ever come across. He could, with just his bare hands, grab a full-grown man by the head, lift him off the ground, and shake him until his neck snapped. To make sure the assassination was completed, he could squeeze the victim's head until the skull bones collapsed. Katrina had seen Vlad kill two men in such a fashion, and it was the most awesome display of raw physical power that she'd ever witnessed.

"Tell the others I'll be there in one hour. Inform Juanita that I'll want my scuba gear ready for me."

Vlad nodded.

The soldiers hurried out of the kitchen. When she was alone, she looked down at her breasts that filled out the silk bodice of her nightgown. Her nipples had become erect, making prominent dents in the snowy white silk. Katrina smiled. Vlad the Impaler had a truly astonishing influence over her body.

Florida Keys, United States

Svetlana Simonov cut the power to the engines and let the rented motorboat cruise to a stop in the gently rolling ocean waves. She was two hundred yards from shore. From her large shoulder bag of woven canvas, she took out a pair of ten-power binoculars and put them to her eyes.

In the distance, she saw the high white marble wall and the three-story mansion nestled away from the oceanfront, surrounded by an enormous green lawn. The residence, thoroughly secluded in a cove, was the ideal place to live for a wealthy man who wanted his privacy. That was the reason that Sir Malcolm Sitwell had purchased the property. But he had been dead for a month. Svetlana was interested in the mansion's new owners.

Svetlana counted at least six men working on one of the two boat houses. There were more of them who had entered the mansion and hadn't come out. Svetlana wondered why so many were necessary.

Two men stepped out of the mansion, and Svetlana adjusted the focus on her binoculars. Even from a distance of two hundred yards, she could see that one of the men was a giant. He towered over the one beside him, and Svetlana had to convince herself that she was looking at two fully grown men, and not a father with his young son walking together.

"Huge . . . got to be seven feet tall," Svetlana murmured. There was something very frightening about the man, even from a great distance. It was more than just his size that was frightening, though Svetlana couldn't precisely define what else it was.

The enormous man seemed to have the respect of the other workers. When he approached them, Svetlana could see that the men worked just a bit more quickly, with greater earnestness.

She saw a flash of light from something off to the east. Svetlana couldn't say why this struck her as odd, but it did, and she turned her attention away from the mansion. She had to refocus her binoculars as she took in the thick trees. There were two homes about a half mile from the mansion, and as Svetlana studied them, she didn't see a soul nearby.

What had she seen in her peripheral vision?

A moment later there was another flash as sunlight reflected off something shiny, but this time Svetlana was able to get a fix on it. There, in the trees, stood two men. Both were Caucasians, casually dressed in loose-fitting cotton shirts and colorful knee-length shorts. One was holding binoculars and the other was standing directly behind him. The man with the binoculars was looking at the mansion that had, until most recently, belonged to Sir Malcolm Sitwell. It was the same mansion that Svetlana had been watching so carefully.

What were two men doing keeping tabs on the mansion? It was clear that they were keeping their presence a secret, since they were staying hidden in the trees. If it hadn't been for the morning sunlight reflecting off the binocular lenses, Svetlana wouldn't have noticed them at all.

"Isn't that interesting?" Svetlana murmured.

Katrina felt the five-inch heels of her stilettos sink into the lawn as she approached the boathouse. She made a mental note to have a concrete walkway put in, one that ran from the mansion to the boathouse, in the near future.

When the three soldiers saw her approaching, every man started to stand at attention, then stopped himself. Old habits were hard to break, and they had been ordered to not stand at attention. They were soldiers for the most secretive — and soon to be the most powerful — criminal organization in the world, and they behaved like it.

"Has the hoist been completed?" Katrina asked, not breaking stride as she walked past Jacques.

"Not yet, Comrade Luvesky," Jacques answered. He turned and followed Katrina into the newly renovated boathouse, with Arturo and Petyr following him. "It will probably be finished later today."

"I don't want to be told what will probably happen," Katrina said as she stepped into the boathouse. "Want I need to know is what will be, not what might be."

"Yes, Comrade Luvesky."

The men had worked around the clock to make the boathouse double its original size. Inside the boathouse, four men were working to bolt together the bracing for an enormous hoist that would, when completed, have the power to lift a small submarine out of the water — which was exactly what it was needed for.

Katrina saw Vlad at the foot of a ladder, holding it steady for Juanita. She was at the top of the ladder, putting a wrench to a stubborn bolt that would not loosen. The ladder wasn't built to withstand the bulk of a man Vlad's size.

"What's wrong?" Katrina asked sharply.

"It's this bolt, Comrade Luvesky," Juanita answered. She turned her attention away from the rafter bolt, down to her superior officer in the Moscow Cartel. "It's rusted, and I can't loosen it. Vlad is too heavy for the ladder."

"Get down," Katrina snapped.

Juanita, looking chastened, descended the ladder. Katrina took the wrench from her and climbed up the ladder. She looked down at Juanita and Vlad. Katrina decided that, after the first successful launch from this boathouse, she would have both Juanita and Vlad at the same time. It would be satisfying to have them simultaneously, one a petite young woman with small breasts and a luscious pink tongue that tantalized, and the other a giant Russian stud with the largest cock Katrina had ever experienced.

Katrina put the wrench on the bolt. After a couple seconds of strain, the bolt broke free with a creaking sound.

"There, now it's loosened," Katrina said as she descended the ladder. "You should strengthen yourself," she told the petite Mexican. "Mr. Bigg does not tolerate weakness—physical, intellectual, or emotional." Katrina was conveniently ignoring that she was physically much larger than Juanita. "I want the hoist completed before nightfall," Katrina said to Vlad the Impaler. "See that I am not disappointed."

The mute Russian nodded silently.

When Vlad turned his gaze toward Jacques, Katrina saw that the giant's eyes were cold as ice. He didn't have to say a word to let the other soldier know that if the hoist was not completed, there would be consequences—fatal ones.

"Juanita, I want you with me," Katrina said.

She turned and headed out of the boathouse as Juanita hurried after her. Katrina had decided that Juanita's educated tongue would be a nice diversion while she waited for Vlad's more penetrating form of pleasure.

Katrina was midway between the boathouse and the mansion when she felt a queer sensation in the pit of her stomach. She immediately stopped walking, and for several seconds stood motionless. She did not look around. She simply tried to get in touch with her own senses.

Something was wrong.

Yes, indeed. Something.

"Comrade Luvesky?" Juanita's voice was barely above a whisper.

"Silence."

Katrina turned and looked at Juanita, then casually turned her attention out to sea. A boat was several hundred yards away. Was there something on the boat that had triggered Katrina's sixth sense? Was the danger out at sea?

Possibly.

A flash of reflected light, off to her left, drew her attention next. The land sloped upward from the water, with a narrow, winding blacktop road leading from the mansion along the oceanfront toward the closest small town some three miles away.

What had caused the flash?

Katrina tried to appear nonchalant, but now the tickle in the pit of her stomach wasn't small and insignificant — it was huge and carried with it a hint of death.

"We're being watched," Katrina said softly. She looked down at Juanita. "I want you to go back to the boathouse. Tell Vlad we're being watched. He'll know what to do."

Katrina looked back into the trees, and this time, when she caught the flash of sunlight reflecting upon a glass lens, she got a fix on the location. There was a man standing against a tree. He was far off, but Katrina's keen eyesight was sufficient to make out his form, as well as the fact that he held binoculars to his eyes.

"Yes, Comrade Luvesky," Juanita said.

Svetlana saw the set-up, and she knew exactly how it was supposed to work. First the enormous man and the petite girl with waist-length black hair moved to the middle of the lawn, where they were clearly visible. Then the girl sank to her knees and began performing fellatio on the giant. Svetlana was too far away to see clearly what she was doing, but from their positions and postures, there could be no confusion about what was happening.

As this was going on, a speedboat eased out of the smaller of the two boathouses. In the speedboat were four men. The boat went at a leisurely speed out of the cove, but once it was in open water, the boat raced northward. When the boat was a quarter mile north of where the men watching the mansion had positioned themselves, the boat pulled up to shore and the occupants hurried out.

The men watching the mansion were now caught between the mansion and the four men from the boat.

"Damn fools," Svetlana muttered aloud when she turned her attention to the binocular-carrying men. They were watching the petite woman on her knees in front of the giant. The two men were even jostling for the binoculars. "You're trapped, and you don't even know it."

She watched as the four men from the mansion approached from behind the two men spying on the mansion grounds. By the time the men with the binoculars realized they were trapped, it was already too late for them to escape.

It wasn't a simple, clean abduction. Not by any means.

Svetlana watched, horrified, as the four men brutally pummeled the other men to the ground, then kicked them mercilessly. For a while Svetlana actually thought the men from the boat were intent upon kicking the other two men to death, but this wasn't the case. Eventually, the two watchers were pushed, kicked, and dragged to the boat.

"Nasty people," Svetlana said as she took the binoculars from her eyes. She turned the key and fired up the Mercury 125 horsepower engine of her rented boat. "Very, very nasty people."

That's the most amazing piece of man-flesh I've ever seen in my life. Katrina watched Juanita struggling to fit Vlad's cockhead into her mouth and wondered if she herself was silly enough to think that she could deep throat a cock that size.

Vlad the Impaler stood with his trousers down to his knees. Juanita was naked from head to toe, kneeling in the grass with her dress on the ground beside her. Katrina was standing at Vlad's side, watching Juanita's performance with rapt attention. Katrina's labia were moist from her pent-up passion. It was only the awareness that someone was paying undue attention to her and the mansion that prevented her from stripping off her dress and letting Vlad the Impaler ravish her right there on the lawn.

It wouldn't be the first time that she'd taken his magnificent cock into her pussy while she had an audience. It wouldn't be the second time. Or even the third.

"You're doing wonderfully," Katrina said to Juanita. She kept her voice a sultry, husky purr of carnality. "It won't be long now before we have those men in custody. Vlad, if these men prove to be dangerous to our operation, I'll be requiring your special services. Would you like that?"

The mute giant nodded. Though he had not broken into a

smile when Juanita began pleasuring him, the joyous thought of killing men in his own special way did pull upward at the corners of his mouth.

"Shall I continue?" Juanita asked, releasing the giant's cock from her oral embrace.

"A while longer," Katrina said. "I don't want him to release, though. I don't want you to satisfy him."

"No, comrade," Juanita replied. "Of course not. Your wish is my command."

"After I have found out what the intruders want, I'll require you," Katrina said to Vlad. She looked up into his face, then down at Juanita. "I'll need both of you. Is that clear?"

Juanita replied, "Yes, Comrade Luvesky." She resumed her pleasuring. As she nibbled on the giant, Juanita reached upward with her left hand, sliding her hand beneath Katrina's skirt, her fingertips skimming lightly against her thigh flesh.

"Save that for later," Katrina snapped harshly. "When I want your caresses, I'll let you know. Until then, Juanita, you do exactly as I tell you. No more, no less."

The girl nodded, her dark brown eyes filled with fear and awe, her mouth filled with Vlad the Impaler.

Federal agents Mervyn Browne and Walter Rodney were jostling each other for the binoculars. Throughout their careers in the Federal Department for Investigating Narcotics Trafficking, they had both seen quite a number of lurid and baffling things. But neither of them had ever watched a beautiful, young, dark-haired girl give fellatio to a massive giant of a man, outside in the middle of the day, with another woman standing nearby watching the whole thing, and, apparently, giving instructions as to what was to be done.

Their assignment was routine enough. Rumors had been going around lately about a new supplier of high-grade cocaine into the United States through the Florida Keys, and somebody somewhere along the chain of command thought there was suspicious activity on the island. Both men had figured the report would be the usual something-might-be-happening-but-we-can't-prove-anything variety. That was, they had thought that until the petite girl willingly sank to her knees and began performing fellatio out in the middle of the mansion's front lawn.

"Come on," Browne complained. "It's my turn. You've had the binoculars long enough."

Rodney shot back, "You had them longer than your turn. Now leave me alone so I can see what she's doing. Why do you figure the tall blonde just stands there without joining?"

"Maybe she's not into threesomes," Browne opined.

"I wonder . . ."

It was the crunch of a shoe on gravel behind them that caught Browne's attention. Browne turned toward the sound just in time to spot the baseball bat at the height of its swing. He raised his arms defensively and was surprised when his attacker neatly brought the bat around to the left, then pulled the swing inward. The thickest part of the baseball bat connected with Browne's ribs, and the sharp *crack* indicated broken bones.

The breath exploded from his lungs and his body convulsed, twisting sideways as savage pain shot through him. He dropped to one knee, one hand clutching his battered side, the other raised over his head to ward off the next blow.

Jacques had other plans. He moved past his first victim, raising the bat again as the second one pivoted to see what was happening. The bat connected with that man's left biceps, nearly breaking his arm and knocking him sideways with such force that he couldn't keep his balance.

With the two men suitably wounded, Arturo, Petyr, and Deiter went to work with fists and feet, putting well-placed punches to stomachs and kidneys, devastating kicks delivered to testicles and chins. In less than thirty seconds, Katrina Luvesky's prime muscle boys within the Moscow Cartel had the federal agents beaten into bloody submission.

CHAPTER FIVE

Katrina Luvesky looked at the two captured men and smiled. They stood in the small tin shed used to house tools and lawn equipment necessary for upkeep of the grounds. The men had their hands bound behind their backs, their ankles tied. Ropes around their necks were attached to the rafters overhead. Should either one lose his balance, he would hang himself.

"Vlad, punch him in the stomach again," Katrina said quietly, looking into Browne's eyes.

Vlad the Impaler dispassionately stepped forward and plowed a ham-sized fist into the federal narcotics agent's solar plexus. Browne doubled over, and when he did, the noose tightened around his neck, causing him to gag and choke as he struggled to regain his breath and his balance.

"You two think you can hold out," Katrina said to the men. "You tell me lies and expect me to believe them. I am a patient woman. I can afford to be. It's not me who has the rope around my neck. When you've stood there three or four hours without moving, standing silently in total darkness as every bone from your ankles on up is aching . . . then we'll see how willing you are to tell me the truth."

A thin sheen of perspiration glowed on Katrina's face and neck. Her nipples were hard pebbles of aroused flesh, making prominent dents in the fabric of her blouse. She loved interrogating suspects with an almost religious intensity. Her clit was throbbing. The lips of her pussy were wet with desire.

"I need a shower," Katrina said to Juanita. "You will help

me with that. Then I'd like to see you and Vlad in my room. Understood?"

"Yes, Comrade Luvesky," Juanita said softly.

The giant Russian killer nodded his mute acceptance.

Svetlana Simonov entered the water, careful to avoid any unnecessary splashing. The sun had gone down twenty minutes earlier, and she had trolled the big Mercury motor until she was within a hundred yards of the shore. She looked at the mansion in the distance, taking note of the lights that were on, the windows that were dark. Earlier in the day she had watched two men being abducted, then later saw them escorted into the small, narrow metal shed. The captives were still inside the shed.

She had to find out for herself if the two abducted men were still alive. If they turned out to be the soldiers of some drug kingpin, then she would turn them over to the authorities, but if they were law enforcement agents, then she'd find out who they were working for, make a discreet call, and quietly bow out of the whole mess after she had gotten them out of danger. Omega Force didn't involve itself in law enforcement operations that were best handled by more traditional agencies.

The water at night was inky black, and Svetlana had to press the luminous dial of her scuba wristwatch against the glass of her mask to see the time and to check the compass on her right wrist. She descended to fifteen feet and began pumping her strong legs slowly and evenly. The long rubber swim fins propelled her smoothly through the water.

Standing, Federal Agent Browne could see only a pinprick of light. He could see it through a crack above the tin door. The single light was all he could see.

But he could feel.

His feet were hurting, and so were his knees. The baseball bat had broken his ribs. The pain in his side from battered bones was only a part of what now ached on him. The tall blonde woman had twice kicked him in the groin after he'd been tied up, his hands bound behind his back, his ankles tied together. Should he lose his balance and fall, he'd hang himself.

It was supposed to be a simple assignment. That was why it had all gone sideways on him, Browne now understood. He had underestimated the danger he and his partner were in. Because of that miscalculation, he had let his defenses down. Now he had some psychopathic woman with icy eyes waiting for his whole body to be just one big ache before she continued with her interrogation.

Browne heard the metal handle of the tin shed turning, and his heart sank in his chest. They were coming back. More horrifyingly, *she* was coming back.

The door opened hardly more than a foot, then a single figure slipped inside. Browne didn't get a good look at her, but he did see enough to know that it was a woman wearing a bikini swimsuit, and that her skin and hair were wet. She came forward, moving slowly. In her right hand was a pistol, with something long and cylindrical attached to the end of it. A silencer? What else could it be? A man in his profession knew about such things.

Browne was now more confused than ever. All he was certain of was that he was in a viper's nest, and that if he ever got out alive, he would go immediately to church and light enough candles and say enough prayers to save his soul a dozen times over.

Svetlana Simonov inspected the men more closely, then went back to the door. She opened it a crack—just enough to allow the light from outside the shed to shine on the men inside. She examined the ropes around their ankles and wrists. Looking Browne in the eyes, she put a finger to her lips. He nodded, and she removed the gag from his mouth.

"What time did they say they'd return?" Her scuba knife made quick work of the coarse hemp ropes.

"She just said *later*. What's your name?" Browne rubbed his ankles and calves, trying to get the circulation going properly once again.

"It's Svetlana. Can you walk? Swim?"

"I can't walk far," Browne said as he helped free Rodney from the ropes. "We're both pretty beaten up."

"I've got scuba gear outside at the water's edge. It's only a single tank, but if we can find life vests for you two, I'll tow you both to my boat."

"Who do you work for?" Browne asked.

"We haven't got time to talk now. Let's move out." Svetlana found two life vests, both sized for children. "These will have to do," she said, handing the vests to the two men. "Don't put them on. Just hang on to them and I'll tow you away from shore. If shooting starts, you'll have to split up. Clear?"

"Clear," Browne replied.

Svetlana took the lead, standing at the tin door, looking out over the expanse of immaculate lawn leading up to the mansion. There was action inside the mansion. Lights glowed in several upstairs windows and in almost all of the downstairs ones.

Svetlana stepped out first. She had her Mauser .32-caliber in both hands, the silencer ready to quiet its explosive roar. The men stepped out of the shed behind her, both limping badly. They walked with the hunched-over posture of men who had been tortured. Svetlana had seen the symptoms before.

Svetlana hurried the men along, moving them away from the shed and toward the water's edge. Her fins, mask, and scuba tank were where she'd left them. She shoved the Mauser into the zippered plastic bag she'd carried the weapon in earlier and slipped her arms into the straps of the scuba tank harness.

"I'll be just beneath the surface," she whispered to Browne. "You two should try to remain as deep in the water as possible. Don't kick or try to swim. Just let me drag you through the water."

Svetlana stepped into the water and put the regulator into her mouth. After adjusting her mask for a proper fit, she crouched in the waist-deep water. Browne held the life vest to his chest. He held Svetlana's right hand. Rodney held onto Browne's ankle.

Pausing a moment, only her head above the surface of the water, Svetlana could hear the sounds of rough-talking men coming from the house. They spoke a language that she could not immediately recognize, though she could tell that the men were moving outside through the shadows, heading toward the shed. Dipping beneath the water, keeping a firm grip on the federal agent's wrist, Svetlana Simonov headed for her rented motorboat, scissoring her long legs.

They reached the boat minutes later. The alarm had yet to sound back at the mansion. The female torturer had been as patient as she claimed she was.

"Who are you?" Rodney asked as Svetlana helped pull him into the speed boat.

"Right now, I'm your guardian angel," Svetlana answered. Her teeth flashed white in the moonlight. "Just relax and let me get us out of here."

Katrina Luvesky was red-eyed furious when she discovered that the captives — *her* captives, she was quick to point out to the men surrounding her — had escaped. She assured every man, and even Juanita, that Mr. Bigg would soon be hearing about the unprofessional breach of security.

"Your failure to perform even the most simple task of maintaining custody of two men, bound hand and foot, will be noted by Mr. Bigg," she whispered, her body quivering with frustration. "If you are to work for the Moscow Cartel, you must not fail. Mr. Bigg considers any failure to be a weakness — a fatal weakness for all of you, should anything like this ever happen again!"

Katrina stepped up to Vlad the Impaler and looked at him. It couldn't be his fault. He had been in the bedroom with Katrina, doing all he could to satisfy her unquenchable sexual desires, when the two men had escaped. And it couldn't be Juanita's fault, either. She had been kissing Katrina's responsive nipples when the foul crime of escape had occurred.

But there were eight other men, all soldiers of the Moscow Cartel, the blame could be pinned to. Would it be better to kill one of those eight now, to make an example of him, or would the threat of Mr. Bigg's displeasure be enough of an incentive to ensure future perfection? Katrina thought about this for a moment before coming to her decision.

"Vlad, come here!"

She snapped her fingers, pointing at the floor directly in front of her feet. Vlad, despite being seven feet tall and weighing over three hundred pounds of solid muscle, hurried to where he had been ordered. Katrina looked up into his eyes, then, with just the slightest nod of her head and the expression in her eyes, indicated that the soldier newest to the Moscow Cartel should die. He was the smallest of the eight men, and Katrina had decided that even though she was slightly undermanned for this all-important operation, discipline—and fear—had to be maintained.

Vlad walked until he was standing behind the young soldier from St. Petersburg. The giant moved quickly but without hurrying. He placed his palms over the boy's ears. For a moment in time, just a mere second or two, the boy's eyes opened wide and he was about to scream. But then Vlad lifted the boy off the ground by his head, and with a sharp twist, left then right, there came the distinct sounds of bones breaking. The soldier's body went limp. Vlad continued holding the corpse off the floor as he began squeezing the head more tightly. Seconds later the corpse's skull collapsed. Blood sluiced from the corpse's mouth and nostrils.

Even the most hardened killers among the soldiers of the Moscow Cartel were horrified at what they had just witnessed.

"That is the price of failure," Katrina said calmly. She gestured toward the corpse dangling in midair, the crushed skull still between Vlad's enormous hands. "See to it that none of you ever forgets this lesson. *I* won't forget. And rest assured, Mr. Bigg will not forget . . . or forgive."

CHAPTER SIX

Katrina wished, for possibly the first time in her adult life, that she wasn't so tall. Her height had always given her an advantage over women — and most men — all her adult life. But inside the mini submarine, her six-foot frame wasn't an asset.

This was the first revelation that came to Katrina as she guided the small, electric-powered craft through the water precisely four feet above the ocean's floor. The second revelation was that, at sixty feet, the water was much, much cooler than at the surface. And since Katrina was only wearing a swimsuit, and the submarine wasn't equipped with the insulation necessary to contain the heat, the submarine was getting frightfully cold.

The dials glowed green and informed Katrina that the submarine's batteries had expended a mere five percent of their full charge, that the vessel was between sixty and sixty-five feet below the surface, that it was cruising at a steady three knots, and most importantly, that the small package a Cessna Skyhawk had dropped from a hundred yards above the water was north by northwest from the submarine's current location.

There was a certain comforting factor in the homing device's continual *ping . . . ping . . . ping*. The sound let Katrina know that the equipment was continuing to pick up the test object's signal, and that she was steadily moving closer to the square plastic box heavily weighted with ten-pound lead bars.

Jacques was in his seat directly behind Katrina. She was glad he was there on this test run, though. As her confidence continued to escalate, she began to wonder whether a second person in the mini submarine was necessary for the pickups. If every exchange went as smoothly as this one, sending two people to pick up the package would be a waste of manpower.

Studying the green-glowing monitors, Katrina judged the test drop site to be less than a hundred yards in front of her. Sometime later, she spotted her target partially buried in the ocean floor — the black plastic box that the Cessna Skyhawk had dropped more than an hour earlier.

"There is it," Katrina said, speaking nearly in a whisper.

Jacques replied in a tone of respectful awe, "Mr. Bigg's plan will work perfectly, Comrade Luvesky."

Katrina was pleased that Jacques couldn't see the self-satisfied smile on her face in the mini submarine. What would he think, she wondered, if he knew that Mr. Bigg was dead and that the entire operation was her idea? Would he be so impressed then, or would he suddenly find flaws in the plan because the mastermind behind the world's most cunning drug-running operation was a woman?

Pushing such questions from her mind — they were immaterial to the problems at hand — she throttled the submarine to a stop less than ten feet from the plastic box. Attached to the box were four white balls made of plastic. The only purpose for the balls was to make the plastic box easier to see, should the homing device not be as effective as Katrina had hoped.

"What now?" Jacques asked.

"Now we leave it here," Katrina answered. "In twelve hours, the batteries will die and the transmitter will stop sending the homing signal. The box itself is filled with nothing but lead weights."

"Yes, Comrade Luvesky." the soldier replied smartly, already reaching for his scuba equipment. "As you command."

Svetlana saw the operation being planned. The men had the look of federal agents. Probably from the Bureau of Alcohol, Tobacco and Firearms, she decided. Maybe the Federal Bureau of Investigations. And their prey was inside the compound.

The men, twenty-six in all, were crowded into a coffee shop in town, three miles from the former estate of Sir Malcomb Sitwell. The uniformity of their appearance — generally tall, mostly Caucasian, in good shape without so much as a single man being truly pot-bellied, every one well-groomed — made up for the omission of any uniform. But Svetlana knew that when the raid on the mansion compound began, they'd all be wearing lightweight navy-blue windbreakers with huge yellow letters stating "ATF" or "FBI."

The men were keeping the waitress at bay, stating they'd get coffee for themselves. And to keep her and the coffee shop's management happy, a half dozen twenty-dollar bills had been palmed over as tips, with sincere promises of more to come if they were given total privacy.

Svetlana wasn't overwhelmingly surprised to see the paramilitary force being assembled. The men she had rescued, no doubt, had placed a call to whomever they answered to. That was why all the soft-spoken men were crowded into the small coffee shop now, going over aerial photographs of Sir Malcomb Sitwell's mansion and grounds.

Svetlana pretended to have trouble finding the ladies restroom, cutting between several of the men. The move allowed her to get a glimpse of the small square table the men were huddled around. Half a dozen photographs were spread out, and a tall unsmiling man was tapping a thick forefinger to one of the photographs, explaining something in hushed tones.

"Where do you think you're going?" a middle-aged man with a rock-hard body asked Svetlana.

"The restroom. Isn't it—"

"It's on the other side," the man replied gruffly, standing to block Svetlana's deeper exploration into their private meeting.

Svetlana gave him a petulant look, turned on her heel, and strode away with her best expression of righteous indignation. Before she stepped out into the bright morning Florida sunshine, an idea struck Svetlana, and it was so daring that she couldn't keep the cunning smile from her lips.

"There must have been twenty of them in the coffee shop," Svetlana said, standing outside the gates of the mansion.

She was talking to a man in his early thirties. He had the hard, unsmiling demeanor of a career soldier who had already seen much bloody death. The man was dressed in khaki trousers and a colorful Hawaiian shirt. He looked like what he was—a soldier making a poor attempt to appear like a tourist. He was, no doubt, wondering why a beautiful woman would drive hurriedly up to the front gate and warn him that "federal men" were planning a raid.

"Inside," the soldier said a moment later, tossing open the lock on the gate. "There's someone you must tell this to."

Svetlana drove her rented Chrysler through the gates, parked it where the man indicated, then stepped out of the car. She was quickly ushered through the grounds and inside the mansion. In what was a spacious and well-appointed library there stood an extremely tall, aristocratic woman with blonde hair. She had striking sea-blue eyes and a demeanor that suggested she could rip a man's throat out with her bare hands and not think twice about it afterward.

The woman introduced herself to Svetlana as Katrina Luvesky. Judging from her bearing, and from the way the men in the room treated her, she was the person in charge, and her slightest wish and whim would be immediately gratified in any way necessary by those around her. The respect she inspired in her underlings would have impressed Svetlana had she not been aware that along with that respect came a truly unhealthy measure of primal fear.

"Why come to me with this?" Katrina asked Svetlana. Her blue gaze went over the Omega Force agent with cool suspicion. "Why concern yourself?"

Svetlana shrugged. "I have an aversion to big government. I had an older brother who got messed up with drugs. The cops saw him trying to make a buy, and when they did, my brother panicked. The cops didn't panic, though. They knew exactly what the hell they were doing when they gunned him down. There was an investigation, but it went nowhere because the cops can't police themselves. So whenever I can take the side of the little person against the government, I always take the little person."

Katrina smiled at that. "You're the first person since I was eleven years old who has called me *little*." She turned away from Svetlana and told the man standing next to her, "Make sure the lawyers are ready. Offer no resistance. We have nothing to hide." She turned her attention back to Svetlana. "What's about to happen has been anticipated, though I appreciate the forewarning you have provided."

"I'll be off, then," Svetlana said, heading for the library door.

"No."

The single word, spoken by Katrina, stopped Svetlana with an almost physical force. She turned to face the Russian.

Katrina smiled, but there was no gentleness in her sea blue eyes. "Stay here. The government men will come, and my lawyers will shred them to pieces. When it is over, then you can leave." She stepped closer to Svetlana, and this time

Katrina's gaze went slowly up and down over the voluptuous blonde. "Please, stay. Be my guest. Accept my hospitality. It's the least I can do for someone who has been so kind."

"If that's what you want . . ." Svetlana replied, not sure whether Katrina had just fallen into her trap, or if it was the other way around.

The ordeal ended shortly after nine PM, when the last of the unmarked sedans drove through the security gates, leaving Katrina Luvesky smiling triumphantly. Two well-paid lawyers had promised a myriad of lawsuits against the United States Government, the Federal Bureau of Investigations, the bureau of Alcohol, Tobacco and Firearms, the Attorney General, and the Immigration and Naturalization Service. There would be more defendants named, but for now, that list would have to do.

The federal agents left with their tails between their legs.

"Would you care for something to eat? Perhaps a little something to drink?" Katrina asked Svetlana. Her voice was a smooth as brushed velvet. "The unpleasantness is over, so let me offer you my hospitality." She smiled softly. "It seems I owe you at least that much." Then, in a softer voice, "Perhaps much more."

Svetlana accepted the offer. What else could she do? She was being held captive inside the walled estate, and even though the mansion was well appointed with every creature comfort, for Svetlana, it was a prison just the same. She could stay willingly, or she could stay unwillingly . . . but she would be staying, one way or the other. Of that fact she had no doubt. She looked at Katrina, taking note of the woman's beauty, and wondered what the evening held in store.

The meal was simple but hearty. Solid American fare, Svetlana thought, amused with the irony of it. She guessed that Katrina was from Russia, perhaps somewhere near St.

Petersburg. Very little remained of her accent. The soldiers were numerous, and Svetlana figured most but not all of them were from former Eastern Bloc countries, probably in the Georgian area of the former Soviet Union.

At the end of the meal, Svetlana and Katrina went back to the library again, taking seats on the long leather sofa. Low wattage table lamps at each end of the sofa were lit, casting a soft glow on both of them.

"I'll send a man for your belongings in the morning," Katrina explained, then took a sip of her vodka martini. "For tonight, I'll find something nice for you to wear. We're pretty much the same body type, though I'm a few inches taller, and you're a bit fuller here." With a hand gesture, she indicated Svetlana's bosom was more ample than her own.

"I can stay at my motel."

"No. You'll stay here tonight. It'll be much more comfortable for you. You've had a traumatic day. You shouldn't be left alone all night." Katrina raised a hand when Svetlana began to protest. "Besides, I have plenty of men here to see to your every need. If you want anything, you just need to ask, and it'll be yours."

Svetlana sipped her gin martini and was marginally displeased with the high percentage of alcohol to vermouth. She could feel Katrina's heated gaze upon her, touching her visually without actually closing the distance that separated them.

They finished their drinks and then went to Katrina's private bedroom to find something for Svetlana to wear. Katrina insisted that Svetlana would be perfectly comfortable in the guest bedroom, though Svetlana strongly suspected that separate beds was not what the mysterious Russian woman had in mind for the end of the evening.

"Here's something that'll fit you, and you'll be lovely in it," Katrina said, displaying a cream-colored silk nightgown she'd taken from her chest of drawers. The neckline dipped into a deep *V* and was embroidered with lace. The garment had slender spaghetti shoulder straps and came down to mid-calf. "Here, put this on for me," Katrina said. "I'm dying to see you in it."

"I'd like to go to my room," Svetlana replied, picking up the nightgown. She noticed that it was heavy silk, and the fine stitching suggested the lingerie was very expensive.

"You can change here, if you like."

"My room is just down the hall."

Svetlana's eyes hinted at submissive acceptance of Katrina's authority, but only if necessary. Svetlana knew the role she was supposed to play.

Katrina smiled. "You're shy. That's nice. There aren't many shy people in the world anymore. Promise me you'll come back? I want to see what you look like in that."

"Here?" Svetlana asked softly. "To your bedroom?"

"That makes you uncomfortable, doesn't it? Very well, meet me in the library." She looked at Svetlana with narrowed eyes. "But don't make me wait long, or I'll be very disappointed with you."

The undercurrent of threat could not be mistaken. Svetlana knew what had been demanded of her.

When she was alone in her own bedroom, Katrina at last let a feline smile spread across her face. She had anticipated trouble when the two captives had escaped, and that was the reason she had her American lawyers on hand and had gotten rid of everything that would in any way suggest illegal activities at the mansion. Nevertheless, Svetlana Simonov's forewarning had been appreciated. As the day wore on and Katrina was able to see Svetlana's sometimes-cool, sometimes-flustered demeanor, she began enjoying the woman's companionship more and more. And it didn't hurt at all that

Svetlana wore a loose-fitting, simple floral blouse that allowed her round breasts to move freely, and a skirt that—though knee-length—gave continual hints there were shapely thighs beneath.

Stripping out of her own clothes quickly, Katrina selected a silk camisole in robin's egg blue for herself. The loose-fitting silk hung from spaghetti straps and came down to the tops of her thighs. She stepped in front of a mirror and looked at herself. When she raised her arms over her head, the bottom hem rose above her thighs. Her pubic hair, trimmed short and in the shape of a triangle, was much darker than the light blonde hair of her head. Katrina momentarily considered putting panties on. She was hungry for a new lesbian conquest, and she was in a hurry to taste feminine flesh. If she had more time, she could be more subtle, more patient and delicately seductive. Circumstances made it necessary to make a bold assault—a blitzkrieg was the only path to quick victory. A direct sexual assault was always in keeping with her temperament.

Stepping to her dressing table, Katrina picked up a bottle of perfume—curiously named Opium—and put a dab upon each wrist, a drop between the swells of her breasts, then a drop at the backs of each knee. Lastly, she stepped into a pair of high-heeled slippers that were the exact shade of light blue as her camisole. The heels pushed her height to four inches over six feet. She would tower over Svetlana now. Katrina was hoping to be impressive, even intimidating, if it achieved the results her body was tingling for.

Katrina returned to the library. She wasn't surprised to find that the room was empty. She made herself a vodka cocktail and fixed a second drink, this one for Svetlana. The drink she made for Svetlana was considerably more potent in alcohol than the one Juanita had previously made for the newest arrival to the unofficial American headquarters of the

Moscow Cartel.

She sat down on the leather sofa, feeling the cool leather against the bare skin of her bottom. She felt a little scandalous walking around the mansion wearing only the shorty camisole without any panties on, but Katrina was feeling bold and daring. She had accurately anticipated what the American government would do, and just that very day she had made the only superpower left in the world look like bungling fools for having invaded her private property. All of this success had made Katrina Luvesky feel supremely confident and overwhelmingly amorous.

Katrina was two-thirds finished with her vodka cocktail before it occurred to her the bitch wasn't going to come to her.

She's going to be damned sorry she didn't follow my orders. Pretty bitches that don't listen to me suffer for it!

And it was precisely at that moment that Svetlana Simonov stepped into the library. She wore the cream-colored nightgown, which clung to her gloriously feminine body. The lingerie defined her curves while simultaneously concealing them. Katrina noted that she had taken a few minutes to touch up her makeup. She'd put a little more lip gloss on a mouth that, to Katrina, seemed as kissable as any she'd ever seen. Katrina was impressed, pleased — and wildly aroused.

"You look stunning," Katrina said, rising from the leather sofa to meet Svetlana halfway into the room.

"Thank you. I was scared someone would see me coming here."

Katrina looked directly into Svetlana's eyes and said with quiet authority, "I gave orders that everyone was to remain in their rooms. We won't be disturbed. No one will see you . . . but me." Katrina eased her arm around Svetlana's bare shoulders. She enjoyed the sensation of smooth flesh beneath her fingertips. "Now, please, come and have another drink with me. I've made you one myself."

Svetlana was barefooted, while Katrina still wore her high-heeled slippers. The Russian soared over Svetlana by a full nine inches. When she looked down, she had a tempting view of Svetlana's fully rounded cleavage.

"I think I've had enough to drink." Svetlana's voice was no more than a whisper. Katrina noted that Svetlana made no effort at all to avoid direct contact. "Cocktails can make me lightheaded."

"Don't worry about being lightheaded," Katrina replied. She pushed the cocktail into Svetlana's hand. "As long as you're with me, you'll be safe. I'll protect you." Katrina had made no effort to hide the possessiveness in her tone.

Svetlana sat on the sofa.

Katrina looked at her, and felt a distinct tingling in her clit. The American who had warned her that the authorities were coming was the very essence of feminine eroticism. Fresh nectar moistened the lips of Katrina's cunt. She hadn't felt quite this way in a long, long time.

When Katrina finally sat on the sofa, she sat so close to Svetlana that their knees touched.

"You'll protect me," Svetlana said softly. She took a sip of her martini, then made a little shiver. She gave Katrina a suspicious look. "But who will protect me from you?"

"You don't need protection from me."

Then, as though to prove quite the opposite, Katrina leaned toward Svetlana. The moment their lips were about to touch, she stopped. She waited as breathless seconds ticked along.

Svetlana finally closed her eyes.

Only then did Katrina kiss Svetlana's full-lipped mouth. It was a soft, gentle, feminine kiss from one woman to another. But the heat it created, the chemistry it ignited, made Katrina Luvesky's passion burn with need. She pressed her mouth more firmly against Svetlana's, and nearly cried with joy when the voluptuous blonde did not back away.

CHAPTER SEVEN

Svetlana felt the hammering of her own heart. She had come to the compound intending on getting a firsthand look at what was going on. She hadn't thought she would end up being a target of seduction for a power-mad Russian woman.

"You didn't pull away," Katrina commented when the brief kiss ended. "I wouldn't like it if you had. It would make me feel as though I'm not wanted, that my concern for your comfort and wellbeing aren't appreciated. I hate feeling unappreciated."

Svetlana looked away. After weighty seconds of silence, she shrugged her shoulders in silent reply. She was well aware that the movement of her breasts, unbound inside the sheer silk bodice of the nightgown, drew the breathless concentration of Katrina Luvesky.

"You are more round than I am," Katrina commented, then casually reached out and ran the tip of her finger along the upper edge of the nightgown's neckline, moving her forefinger from one breast into the perfumed valley, and then to the other breast.

Her touch was light as a feather. It was intensely erotic.

Svetlana's heart skipped a beat, and her mouth went instantly dry. She looked down at the finger touching her just above the edge of her bodice, and a myriad of chaotic feelings shot through her system. Svetlana, desperate to dampen the seductive mood in the room, said jokingly, "Round? That's just a nice word for fat, right?"

"Not at all, darling. See how your breasts fill out the bodice so nicely? What are you? A double-D cup?"

"A single D."

"Better still. There is such a thing as too much of a good thing, even if men don't realize it. And you're natural. I could tell that hours ago." Katrina chuckled softly, throatily, the sound like a sensual purr. "I can almost always tell at a glance, even if a woman's wearing a proper brassiere. I know what's from nature and what's from a doctor."

She took her hand away from Svetlana's bosom and sighed with a certain mournfulness, as though no longer touching the velvety pale flesh was cause for sadness.

"You're not drinking." Katrina touched her fingertips to the underside of Svetlana's martini glass, nudging the crystal closer to her full-lipped mouth. "I don't want to drink alone. It says such a terrible thing about a woman if she drinks alone."

Svetlana sipped her martini. It was very dry. The liquor was eighty proof. She looked at Katrina, and though she had tried to keep her gaze away from the woman's long, naked legs, she couldn't keep from glancing downward. When she gazed up into Katrina's face afterward, Svetlana thought she detected a certain twinkle of triumph in the Russian's cool gaze.

"What was all that about today?" Svetlana asked. She knew she had to be careful of the questions she asked. "Those government men . . .they seemed quite certain of themselves. What did they think you'd done?"

Katrina's gaze hardened. "I'm going to explain something to you, but I'm only going to tell you this once. Government men always act as though they are quite certain of themselves, and they invariably think that someone has done something wrong. It's by thinking that way that they *become* government men. It doesn't make any difference which government or which country you're talking about. They're the same everywhere. It's like some terrible disease that multiplies all by itself, like a cancer. There, now that I've explained that, we can close the door on those awful men." Katrina touched her glass lightly to Svetlana's. "A toast! To new friendships! And to the victors!"

"To the victors," Svetlana said, and took a sip.

"Not to new friendships?" There was an injured quality in Katrina's tone.

Svetlana touched her glass to the tall woman's and gave her a smile. She added, "To new friendships, of course."

Svetlana took another sip of her martini, looking at her hostess over the rim of the glass. Svetlana was certain that the leggy Russian woman was up to something illegal. Why else would she have an army of lawyers at her beck and call? But what that illegal enterprise was, Svetlana didn't know. Did Katrina's secret plans have anything to do with the alleged murder-slash-suicide of Sir Malcomb Sitwell and his family?

"I'd better be going," Svetlana said, pushing herself off the sofa. She stood barefooted, looking down at an obviously annoyed Katrina Luvesky. "It's very late, and this has been a terribly trying day."

Remaining seated, Katrina reached out and curled her fingers lightly into Svetlana's hand. Her gaze trailed slowly up Svetlana's body until she was looking into Svetlana's eyes. She asked, "Must you really?" When Svetlana nodded, Katrina added, "In that case, I will, like a good hostess, allow you to retire for the evening. I will walk you to your bedroom."

"That's not necessary."

There was a momentary iciness in Katrina's tone as she said slowly, "My dear, I insist . . ."

Svetlana sensed that Katrina's murderous temper was kept in check only by a conscious act of willpower. She wondered what happened when the Russian autocrat let her temper have free rein with the people who worked her for. The images that came to mind were enough to make Svetlana shiver.

"You tremble." Katrina rose swiftly to her feet. She towered over Svetlana, standing so close that the tips of her breasts nearly touched Svetlana's. "Forgive me. I guess I'm so used to conflict in my life that I forget how much it can disturb a gentle soul such as yourself." Katrina took Svetlana's hand and gave it a comforting squeeze. "Let me walk you to your room. In the morning, everything will look much brighter. I promise."

They walked out of the library together. Svetlana felt self-conscious. She was wearing a nightgown that hugged her body like a second skin, with a bodice that was slightly too small, which made her feel jittery inside. She was also holding hands with another woman. Svetlana had in the past enjoyed sex with other women, but it was a pleasure that she wasn't entirely comfortable with. Sex with another woman was a guilty pleasure for Svetlana, with not-always-equal measures of pleasure to go along with the guilt that invariably followed. Also playing on her mind was the fact that the house was filled with men. Would she be *given* to those men if she resisted Katrina's advances? A thousand unanswered questions bounced around in her brain. But she was intrigued. Oh, yes. Very, very intrigued.

"You have a lovely home," Svetlana heard herself say. Silence was difficult for her now that the Russian woman's amorous inclinations had become glaringly obvious.

"We haven't been here long."

"We?" Svetlana felt Katrina stiffen at the question. "You mean the workers who are fixing the place up for you?" Svetlana added, intentionally giving Katrina an easy answer. This was not the time to trigger the woman's paranoia. Not when Svetlana was on the trail of whatever scheme her Russian hostess had in the works.

"Yes. Yes, of course. I mustn't forget about the workers."

Svetlana eased her hand out of Katrina's, but she had to do it against some resistance. As she walked, her bare feet soundless against the thick carpeting in the hallway, she listened for other people in the house. She couldn't hear a thing. Nothing but dead silence. It was an eerie revelation to know that everyone else in the house was so frightened of Katrina's wrath that when she ordered them all to stay in their rooms and remain completely quiet, that was exactly what they did. In a corner of Svetlana's mind she could picture grown men huddled in darkened rooms, too fearful of Katrina to even leave a light on.

They reached her guest bedroom. The door was open. Svetlana looked into the room at the queen-sized bed and saw that the blankets had been turned back. It was only then, standing near the doorway to her bedroom, that Svetlana realized she still held her martini glass in her hand.

"Good night," she said, turning toward Katrina. The situation was an awkward one for Svetlana. She knew that Katrina wasn't going to give up her plans for seduction easily, but the more that Svetlana learned about the Russian, the more frightened she was of her.

"You're sure there's nothing else that you need?"

"Nothing. I'll be perfectly comfortable."

"Finish your martini. It'll help you sleep."

"I've already drunk more than I should."

Katrina put her fingers once more to the underside martini glass and raised it, pushing it upward to Svetlana's mouth. Svetlana thought of resisting, but a glance into Katrina's eyes warned her that she mustn't. The martini was extremely strong, and Svetlana had to swallow three times before she'd finished it all. Only then, when she'd drunk the last drop, did Katrina allow Svetlana to move the glass from her mouth.

"Now you'll sleep as peaceful as a beautiful baby," Katrina

purred. She finished the last of her own cocktail, and then extended the glass to Svetlana. "Hold this for me, will you?"

Svetlana took the glass, asking, "Why?"

Katrina's tone was diamond-hard as she replied, "Because I told you to."

The approach was slow and precise. Katrina very carefully and deliberately wrapped the fingers of her right hand around Svetlana's slender left wrist, then did the same with the other hand. Svetlana was confused. She looked into the tall woman's eyes—and in those icy depths she saw a steely determination that had as much to do with megalomania as with lust.

Katrina raised Svetlana's hands to shoulder height and pinned her wrists against the wall. When Svetlana gasped, startled at what the Russian had done, Katrina chuckled lustfully. Once again, for several weighty seconds, the two women looked into each other's eyes. It was Svetlana who looked away first.

"I frighten you, don't I?" Katrina asked. "You do not need to be frightened of me." She chuckled again. "Or maybe you should." She sighed softly. "You can't imagine the behavior I'm capable of."

She leaned closer to Svetlana and bent her knees enough that her breasts were at the same height as Svetlana's. Leaning closer still, she pressed her bosom against Svetlana's, prompting Svetlana to let out another startled exclamation.

"You're not frightened, are you, my dear?"

Svetlana's mind was in a whirl. She didn't know what role to play. Did Katrina want her to act like a frightened virgin who had never experienced passion with another woman before? Or did she want her to match aggression with aggression, fiery passion with fiery passion? It was a question that only time would answer, and Svetlana suspected that the consequences of choosing the wrong role to adopt could be severe.

Katrina moved up and down several times, then from side to side, rubbing her breasts against Svetlana's larger bosom.

Svetlana was breathing deeply, her eyes moistening. The tips of her breasts were as hard as little pebbles. Hot tingles were shooting from her nipples throughout her body. Svetlana cursed herself for becoming so aroused because of Katrina's forceful assault upon her libido. Svetlana decided against making any effort to be Katrina's equal in the seduction. When Katrina leaned forward, attempting to kiss Svetlana on the mouth, Svetlana turned her face away. "Katrina . . .please . . ." she whispered.

Svetlana's nipples were burning. She attempted to move her wrists away from the wall, but Katrina held her tightly. Svetlana realized that the Russian was very strong for a woman. Svetlana felt helpless but thoroughly excited. She was trapped as much by Katrina's allure as by her sheer physical strength. At the juncture of her own thighs, Svetlana could feel that she was heated and moist. Even if her better judgment was against what was happening, Svetlana's body — acting on impulses primal and indiscriminate — was ecstatic over the way it was being treated.

"One kiss," Katrina continued, her breath warm against Svetlana's cheek. Using the tip of her tongue, she traced the shell-like circumference of Svetlana's ear. "One kiss goodnight, and I'll let you go."

"You've already kissed me."

"That wasn't much of a kiss. You didn't really kiss me back. I need one good kiss before I can let you go."

Svetlana could literally feel her own heartbeat pulsing in her clitoris. When Katrina moved her shoulders from side to side, rubbing her breasts against Svetlana's, the lusty sensations this evoked caused her legs to tremble and her knees to weaken.

"I just need to taste one good kiss." Katrina laughed softly and gently bit Svetlana's earlobe. "Or are you afraid that after one good kiss, you'll want more? You're afraid that once you start with me, you won't be able to stop. That's it, isn't it? Admit it, Svetlana. Admit that I make you weak!"

In a barely audible whisper, Svetlana breathed the words, "Stop it!"

Continuing to hold Svetlana's wrists against the wall, Katrina leaned back and raked her gaze over Svetlana's body. Uttering an obscenity in Russian, Katrina dipped her head. Opening her mouth wide, she captured as much of Svetlana's left breast between her lips as she could, sucking hard on the tender flesh through the barrier of the silk nightgown.

Svetlana gasped. She tossed her head backward so sharply it banged loudly against the wall. She squeezed her eyes tightly shut. The warm wetness of Katrina's mouth surrounding the crest of her sensitive breast matched the heat moistening Svetlana's most private place. Svetlana tried once more to pull her wrists free from the Russian's. Just like before, she could not get her wrists away from the wall. When Katrina transferred her lusty attention to Svetlana's right breast, a fresh surge of carnal excitement shot through the secret agent.

Katrina worked Svetlana's nipples into a fiery state of erection, then cruelly bit each excitable button of flesh through the nightgown, intentionally causing as much pain as pleasure.

"Ouch! That hurts!" Svetlana whispered. There wasn't much criticism in her tone.

Katrina chuckled, then pressed her mouth firmly into the extravagant mound of Svetlana's right breast. She bit Svetlana's nipple again—even harder this time.

"You're hurting me!"

"You want me to hurt you!"

"I don't!"

"Then kiss me. One kiss and I'll set you free!"

Svetlana looked into Katrina's fiery eyes. The Russian, nearly a half-foot taller by nature and made even taller with the high-heeled slippers, dipped her head down, her lips slightly parted.

She's going to kiss me. Svetlana could not say with any certainty whether this was a good or a bad thing, whether it was exciting or loathsome.

Katrina's lips were an inch from Svetlana's when Juanita ran around the corner of the stairway, into the hallway.

"Comrade Luvesky! There's something I must . . ."

Juanita's words trailed off as she discovered just exactly what she had interrupted.

Katrina released Svetlana's wrists.

Still holding the glasses, Svetlana immediately crossed her arms over breasts, hiding the wet spot at the crest of each mound caused by the lusty kisses and tantalizing punishment she had received there.

"What is it, Juanita?" Katrina demanded. She put her hands on her hips and glared down at the short girl.

"I must show you," Juanita answered, quietly but with determination. "It is what the men left behind. I think they are bugs."

Katrina frowned, not understanding the American slang. "Bugs?"

"Listening devices."

Katrina uttered a string of Russian obscenities. Svetlana understood only some of the words.

"Wait for me in the kitchen," Katrina said to Juanita. "Who knows of this?"

"Just you, Comrade Luvesky."

"Good. Keep it that way for now." Katrina turned toward Svetlana. "I'm sorry, but you're going to have to go back to your motel. Those government men that were here earlier have created some problems that I must solve. Stay in your motel room until I call you." Her lips pursed tightly for a moment. She said softly, "This is not the way I wanted this evening to end."

Katrina Luvesky could feel a murderous wrath building within her chest. She wanted desperately to kill someone. Specifically, she wanted to kill an American. She wasn't even picky about which American, so long as she could kill him slowly. She wanted the victim aware that he was going to die. She wanted him to beg for the end to come mercifully swift, but that would be something she would not deliver. Death would come by inches, and she'd be looking into his eyes when it finally came.

The rage was caused by the discovery of a listening device, a "bug" no larger than the tip of Katrina's finger. Juanita had found the bug in her bedroom, beneath her telephone. With some searching, Katrina found a second miniature listening device in her own bedroom. The third, fourth, and fifth bugs were found in the library.

"If we've found five, they've probably put fifty in the house," Katrina said, bending low so that she could whisper into Juanita's ear. "What I need to figure out is who *they* are. You can't fight an enemy when you don't know who and what he is. Let the men all know that they mustn't say anything aloud that might incriminate us."

"Will this cause you to alter your plans, Comrade Luvesky?"

"No. This is but a minor problem."

Juanita smiled. "That is good, Comrade Luvesky. I knew that you were smarter than those men."

Katrina was in her bedroom, sitting at the edge of her bed. Her makeup was complete. She wore an exquisitely tailored pants suit, very mannish in nature, charcoal gray in color, and pinstriped.

"Let's try the black pumps," Katrina said. "Those'll go with my necktie."

"Yes, Comrade Luvesky," Juanita replied.

Juanita was at the entrance to the walk-in closet. She found Katrina's black pumps. Open-toed and with a three-inch heel, they would make the Katrina taller and more impressive than she already was. Juanita got the shoes and brought them over to Katrina. The girl knelt and gently eased the shoes onto Katrina's feet.

Katrina looked at herself in the mirror. She liked what she saw. Six-foot-three in height, wearing a masculine gray pinstriped suit with a white shirt and a black silk necktie. She appeared even taller when standing next to a bare-footed, petite girl barely five feet tall and hardly weighing a hundred pounds. When she met with her American distributor, the Mafia kingpin who promised that he could move five hundred kilograms of pure cocaine a week, Katrina would have Vlad beside her. Between the seven-foot Vlad and the six-foot-three-in-heels Katrina Luvesky, they would be an intimidating duo.

"Have Vlad bring the car out front," Katrina ordered, speaking in a normal tone. She leaned down so that her lips were close to Juanita's ear and added, "And tell the soldiers to be on alert, and to keep silent. The walls have ears."

Svetlana was dressed in black from head to toe. She had chosen to once again spy upon Katrina Luvesky's property from the sea, though she had a different rented boat this time. It was an ancient affair that was perfectly seaworthy, but it wouldn't draw even the slightest bit of interest from anyone. And that was exactly the way Svetlana wanted it.

What was going on at the former residence of Sir Malcomb Sitwell? Svetlana didn't have the evidence to inform Jefferson Burke that she knew, beyond a doubt, that Sir Malcomb had been murdered instead of committing suicide, as the official report claimed. But Svetlana knew in her heart that Sir Malcomb had been a good man, and Katrina Luvesky—called *Comrade Luvesky* by her young Mexican servant—was no innocent woman who had simply stumbled upon a hot piece of property in southern Florida. Whatever had happened to Sir Malcomb was somehow intractably linked with Katrina Luvesky. Svetlana felt it in her bones, even though she didn't have a single shred of evidence to support her opinion.

I don't know what she's up to, but whatever it is, it's no good. It's evil to the core.

Svetlana watched as a vehicle made a wide circle from the front entrance, then sped through the arched gateway.

"Now where the hell do you suppose she's going?" Svetlana murmured aloud, following the vehicle with her binoculars until she could no longer see it.

Svetlana started the engine of her rented boat, though she really didn't know where she would go. All she was certain of was that she needed a better look at what was in place at Katrina's homestead. Whatever was happening, whatever plans Katrina had going, were linked to the land . . .and though Svetlana didn't have one iota of evidence to suggest it, she believed that Sir Malcomb Sitwell had been murdered because of the property that he owned, not because of the man that he was.

Alberto Sacci had kicked, clawed, murdered, and double-crossed his way into being the most powerful Mafia kingpin of the southeastern United States, and he wasn't used to people being late for a meeting with him. *He* was often late. It showed whoever he was dealing with that he was the boss, the one to write all the rules, and that he was above the rules. But nobody was ever late for a meeting with him. It just wasn't done.

He looked at his wristwatch. It was a gold Rolex with enough diamonds in it to blind a man in bright sunlight. The man who had given it to him said it was a gift to commemorate what he was certain would be a long and profitable business partnership. A year later, Sacci's top hitman ended the partnership with a .357 Magnum. Alberto Sacci didn't mind going in business with people, but he hated any fool thinking that it was an equal partnership. That was why he ordered the execution of the man who had given him the diamond-laden gold Rolex.

"They're here!"

Alberto looked again at his wristwatch. The Russian was exactly fifteen minutes late, and this made the Mafia don grit his teeth. Fifteen minutes on the nose meant that was exactly how long the Russian had intended on keeping him waiting.

"Let 'em in," Alberto Sacci said to his soldier.

For the meeting with the leaders of the Moscow Cartel, Alberto had chosen the back room of a seafood restaurant on the cove. It was private, and best of all, he knew that he could speak without worrying about being recorded. Alberto had been good friends with some of the New York Mafia leaders who had gotten nailed by the Department of Justice, and he knew how incriminating video tapes and audio tapes were in a court of law, especially when the government was trying to invoke the stiff racketeering penalties.

Alberto Sacci's next thought was *That's the tallest broad I've ever seen in my life. And the guy with her has gotta be seven fucking feet tall!*

None of this showed in Alberto's expression as he rose from his chair and extended a hand.

"Alberto Sacci."

"Katrina Luvesky. This is my assistant, Vlad. He doesn't speak."

"That's fine by me. Truth is, I wish some of my boys couldn't speak. That way they always got their listening ears on." Alberto sat back down in his chair. With a wave of his hand, his two men, along with Vlad, crossed to the opposite side of the room and took chairs. "I told you right up front that I only deal with the top man." The Mafia don's tone was accusatorial. "Top man sure as hell ain't that mute giant you got over there, and it ain't you. This ain't a way to start a business relationship."

"You have heard of Mr. Bigg, the leader of the Moscow Cartel. I am Katrina Luvesky. I am his lover, his right hand, his most trusted advisor, his confidante, his closest ally, his best friend. He cannot be here this evening, but you can rest assured that everything I say has his blessings. Any agreement we come to here tonight will be considered an agreement with Mr. Bigg." Katrina crossed her legs at the knee before inspecting the fingernail polish on her left hand. She was glaringly unfazed by Alberto Sacci's anger. When she looked up again, her gaze was cool. "A pipeline is in place that will transport one hundred kilograms of ninety-five percent pure cocaine into the country. We have discussed all this in the past, and what had been a dream six months ago is now a reality. Are you still interested in being the purchaser of that cocaine? And can you provide the proper funding for the merchandise?"

Alberto Sacci was taken aback by the leggy Russian with the imperious manner. People didn't talk down to him. Nobody. And sure as hell not some woman he'd just met.

"Now listen—"

"No, you listen!" Katrina shot back. It was the first time she'd raised her voice or moved quickly, and the effect was startling. There was suddenly fire in her icy blue eyes. She leaned closer to Sacci, though she kept her voice low enough that their subordinates across the room could not hear her. "The Moscow Cartel can deliver product which will make you a billionaire within two to three years. You know that's true because you're a smart man, and after the last time we talked, you did the math. With that many kilograms of pure cocaine, you can buy the politicians and the police protection that'll make you the undisputed leader of the most powerful Mafia family in the United States." She paused a moment to look directly into Sacci's eyes. He looked away, but for only a moment. "You've got competition in Philadelphia and in San Diego. Those are powerful men, and they're just waiting for you to make a mistake before they move against you. With the profits from our partnership, you can destroy those men. Philadelphia and San Diego will be yours, not theirs. Once you consolidate their power into your own, you can make your move on New York." Katrina's mouth quirked into a half-smile as though what she was about to say was superfluous. "Once you own New York, you own the world."

Alberto Sacci had never heard of a woman being any Mafia don's most trusted advisor, but what this woman said rang with truth. Besides, Julio the Snake in San Diego had been a pain in the rear end for a long time now. It would be nice to have the clout to order a contract out on him.

Alberto said, "If we get this thing going, I gotta have the stuff regular as clockwork. These things work only as long as everyone knows what's expected of them and everyone does his job."

"Mr. Bigg agrees completely. That's why I can guarantee that you will have your shipment every week."

"Guaranteed?"

"Guaranteed."

Alberto Sacci leaned back in his chair, giving the tall

Russian woman a critical once-over. When word first started through the grapevine that there was going to be a new supplier for top-notch, hard-core drugs into the United States, Sacci had been curious, but nothing more than that. He'd heard such rumors before. Then he heard that the supplier was coming out of Russia, and that a partnership had been formed with a South American drug kingpin to form the Moscow Cartel, and Sacci began giving the rumor more credibility. The more he learned, the more he believed in the Moscow Cartel.

"This ain't the way I usually do business," Sacci said after a moment. "I always deal with the top man and nobody else."

"Mr. Bigg cannot be here, but he wants you to know that as soon as possible, he will meet with you personally. He does apologize for his absence, and hopes that you'll be generous enough to overlook this inconvenience."

Sacci looked over at Vlad, then at his men, then back to Katrina. He said quietly, "That big man of yours stands out like a sore thumb. Hard to keep someone like him from drawing attention from the cops."

"I bring him out only when I need him. Otherwise, he's kept under wraps. But that's my concern, not yours. Do we have an agreement?"

Alberto Sacci didn't particularly like shaking hands with women, but he leaned forward and shook Katrina's hand. Then, to his soldiers, he said, "Go to the trunk and get the dough. We got us a business agreement."

Five minutes later, Katrina Luvesky, leader of the Moscow Cartel, walked out of the restaurant with Vlad at her side. She carried a briefcase filled with five hundred thousand dollars in twenties, fifties, and hundred-dollar bills. It was the *seed money,* a small down payment necessary to get the pipeline started. The smile that tugged at Katrina's mouth was only partially concealed as she stepped out of the restaurant's banquet room with Vlad the Impaler at her side.

All her dreams were coming together. All the plans that Mr. Bigg had made were finally coming to fruition. The U.S. government had already made fools of themselves by invading her home complex — they'd have to think once and twice and three times before they did that again.

Thank goodness for Svetlana, Katrina thought as she paused to allow Vlad to open the rear door of the Chevrolet Suburban. *The forewarning she gave me about the raid made all the difference in the world!*

Port Santa Ruiz, Cuba

Tito Castillo knew he was going to be in trouble when he got home. His wife hated it whenever he was out late. She always assumed that he was drinking rum and playing cards. More times than not when he was late, her fears were justified. But this night was different. This night he was double- and triple-checking his ancient fishing boat. He had been given an assignment that had come directly from a close assistant to El Presidente. Castillo had been told that El Presidente himself had approved of the plan. Since Castillo adored his leader, he wanted to make sure that his old boat, which desperately needed a thorough going-over with paint, as well as some hull work, would be up to the service the Revolution expected of him.

The assignment was simple enough. Appear to be a Cuban fisherman — which would be easy, since that was exactly what Castillo was — and leave port in the morning. Stop three miles out to sea, and stay there. Wait until he received a radio message that he was to proceed, and from that point forward, follow his charts and his LORAN readings exactly.

At precisely fifteen miles off the Florida Keys, he was to

press the button which would release the cargo that he had been towing with him. The cargo had been attached when he'd anchored off the coast of Cuba. From that point forward, Castillo had been towing the cargo fifteen feet below the surface of the water. Should he be stopped by the United States Coast Guard, he was to press the release button. The cargo would sink to the ocean floor in its weighted, watertight container, and be retrieved later.

If there were no problems with American authorities, then Castillo was to pilot his old and thoroughly benign-looking fishing boat off the coast of Florida, drop his cargo at precisely the location he had programmed into his LORAN unit, then turn around and motor slowly back to Cuba.

Castillo had been assured that El Presidente approved of what was being done. Furthermore, Castillo had been told that he would receive a huge bonus—in United States dollars—for his loyalty and duty to the Revolution.

All he had to do was follow the charts, follow the LORAN headings, and do exactly as he had been instructed. And then, once he'd completed his assignment, never talk about it to anyone. Not even his wife. Not to any of his eleven children. If he kept the secret, Castillo might be allowed to do more such runs to the Florida coast in the future.

But he had to keep his mouth shut. And if he didn't . . .

Tonight, his good wife would give him hell for coming home late without having an excuse. But soon, when he showed her a fistful of American twenty dollar bills, then she would know that there were times when her good husband simply had to keep his actions a secret, and that if she was a good wife, she would keep her questions to herself.

Soon. Very soon.

CHAPTER EIGHT

Katrina stood quietly near the mini submarine. She was alone in the boathouse, as she wanted to be. She was on the verge of collecting her first shipment of ninety-five percent pure cocaine. Once the entire fields-to-street-distribution network was working smoothly, she calculated that her personal take should be no less than three hundred million dollars a year. Probably much more than that.

The agreement she'd come to with the Mafia the previous evening was the final piece to the puzzle that had needed to be put in place. Even with the expenses incurred in running the Moscow Cartel, her net worth, within forty-eight months, should be no less than a one-point-five billion.

She glanced at her wristwatch. It was nine PM. The scheduled time for her to leave in the mini sub was ten o'clock sharp. The water would be black as ink, and she would need to navigate strictly with her instruments, but she wasn't in the least concerned with this. The homing device used in the underwater containers had been tested and tested again. A person didn't put one hundred kilograms worth of pure cocaine into a box without knowing exactly how watertight the box was, as well as making sure that the box could be found once it sank to the bottom of the ocean.

The pickup place would put Katrina in one hundred feet of water. This time she wouldn't wear her bikini and end up shivering. She'd wear street clothes—jeans and a pullover sweater—and be perfectly comfortable. And she'd take Juanita with her instead of Jacques. She enjoyed Juanita's company much more, and since the second person in the sub only had to be there in case of emergency — and Katrina had planned and re-planned the operation so many times she knew there wouldn't be any emergencies — she might just as well spend the three hours with someone she enjoyed being near.

Besides, Katrina was already planning a victory celebration that featured herself as the main attraction. The secondary role players, whose job was to make sure that she, as the leader of the Moscow Cartel, was given as much erotic attention as she was capable of withstanding, were Juanita, Vlad the Impaler, and Svetlana Simonov.

Though she was looking at the gleaming silver metal exterior of the mini-submarine, Katrina's thoughts were looking forward toward the celebration. In her mind's eye she could picture herself in a king-sized bed, with Juanita at one side of her and Svetlana at the other. Vlad the Impaler would be front and center, of course.

Katrina looked at her wristwatch and smiled again. Somewhere far out to sea, a Cuban fisherman was piloting his boat slowly and steadily toward Florida. Drifting beneath his harmless-looking old boat, attached by a chain, was a rectangular plastic box, loaded with weights and fitted with electronic transmitters. When the fisherman reached the pre-fixed LORAN setting, he'd release the cargo, which would then sink one hundred twenty feet to the ocean floor. The fisherman would return slowly to Cuba, and Katrina would begin an operation that would make her a billionaire.

There was a soft knock at the boathouse door. A moment later Vlad stuck his head inside. He looked at Katrina, then extended his left arm and pointed to his wristwatch.

"You're right, Vlad, it is time to prepare the submarine. Get the men on it right away. I want to be leaving here at precisely twenty-two-hundred hours."

Vlad nodded and closed the door.

Billionaire. That had a nice sound to it. Katrina thought it would sound especially nice when attached to her name. She turned and headed out of the boathouse. Her men knew what was expected of them, so she didn't have to oversee the readying of the mini-sub.

Everything was going according to plan.

Everything.

"Hatch secured," Juanita stated.

"Confirmed."

Katrina looked to her left, out the porthole, as the submarine slipped beneath the surface of the water. She always got a charge of adrenaline whenever she first took the sub beneath the surface. She flipped a toggle lever. She watched navigation and equipment monitor dials come alive, jerking left to right and vacillating until they settled on the proper reading. The single propeller whirred softly, and the sub started forward, moving at a depth of ten feet, heading out of the cove.

All around, the water was midnight black.

The sonar beeped softly, steadily. The dull green glow of the instrument panel gave Katrina a reading of what was ahead of her, what was beneath her. The sonar was sensitive enough to pick up medium-sized fish. As she turned the craft southward, into the Florida Straits, a mako shark cruised slowly along with the submarine, eyeing it warily. Katrina could not see the shark, only its presence on her sonar screen.

You're a predator, but so am I. Katrina watched the sonar image of the shark swimming out of view. *These are your waters, but I'm at the top of the food chain. I'm the alpha predator. Don't ever forget that, my water-breathing friend. Not if you want to live.*

Svetlana was sitting in an elm tree, remaining motionless,

only her focus moving slowly left to right, then back again. She wore black from head to toe. Black jeans, lightweight black turtleneck sweater, black athletic shoes, and black stocking cap.

She needed to make a closer investigation of Katrina Luvesky's compound. She wanted to see what else was going on in the new boathouses that many men had erected so quickly. She wanted to see what mischief was going on in the basement and attic and in all the nooks and crannies of the tall Russian woman's home. It was in the home that Svetlana was certain she would find the truth to Sir Malcomb Sitwell's murder.

Svetlana no longer thought of the Englishman's demise in terms of murder-slash-suicide. There was too much circumstantial evidence indicating foul play, and her sixth sense was whispering there was *very* foul play in action. Somewhere on the property was the evidence Svetlana needed to learn what enterprise Katrina had going.

Svetlana had concluded that the Russian woman had a grand scheme. That Katrina ruled with an iron fist, she had witnessed firsthand. That Katrina was extraordinarily wealthy was obvious enough. That she was spending heavily to renovate the compound was also evident. But why spend so much money on a place that was already surrounded by a high concrete wall?

From the holster under her left arm, Svetlana plucked out her Mauser HSc, chambered for .32-caliber ammunition. The seven rounds in the first magazine were not typical copper-jacketed hollow-points. The first seven rounds carried ammunition made by munitions experts at Omega Force. The rounds packed very little gunpowder, and rather than firing a lead bullet, they fired a drug-impregnated dart. The drug—Hexoral—caused instantaneous but temporary paralysis. Twenty seconds after paralysis, the victim was unconscious, and stayed that way for some time. Jefferson Burke of Omega Force had dubbed the ammunition *Sleeping Beauty.* He did have a sense of irony.

From a small canvas bag slung over one shoulder, she extracted the titanium and alloy Omega Force silencer and carefully fitted it to the muzzle. In her back-left pocket she had an additional four magazines, each loaded with seven rounds of lethal hollow points. In her back-right pocket she carried the palm-sized Colt Junior in .25-caliber. It was a miniaturized version of the famous Government Model 1911 .45. Svetlana had no extra ammunition for that weapon. Should the fighting ever get down to that, if she couldn't get herself to safety with six rounds from *Junior,* she simply wasn't going to get to safety.

Also in the canvas bag was a miniature camera with special film which allowed it to be used in extremely low light, three stun grenades that caused noise and flash but very little physical damage, and if things got really bad, five baseball-sized fragmentation grenades that shook the earth when they exploded and sent deadly double-ought buckshot flying in all directions. The grenades were an ugly, indiscriminate weapon.

She had scoped the place out carefully and decided that for this insertion into enemy territory, water was not the best way to arrive. The soldiers — and Svetlana now saw the men surrounding Katrina as professional mercenaries, not as workmen — were keeping a careful eye out toward the water. Before sundown, a man had been stationed at the water's edge, looking out. He hadn't moved. Svetlana had previously been introduced to him. His name was Deiter. When nightfall came, Arturo took his place. Deiter went into the mansion, and Arturo stayed outside near one of the boathouses, chain-smoking non-filtered cigarettes and looking bored.

Svetlana had found what appeared to be the most

vulnerable point of the encampment. It was here that the sur-rounding wall had, over the years, been overrun by a tall elm tree. The tree had recently been pruned, its lower branches near the eight-foot wall cut away. But whoever had done the work had not bothered to do a first-rate job of it. He hadn't cut away all the branches that could be used as a perch to in-vade the property.

They weren't such professionals after all, Svetlana thought as she sat on the branch that was closest to the wall.

Inside the mansion, a curtain was up and lights were on. Four soldiers were playing cards. Svetlana recognized Jacques. She knew he was the highest-ranking soldier, be-cause when he slapped a man less than good-naturedly on the back, he laughed about it and the clearly offended soldier did nothing back — at least not right away. A few minutes later, when the soldier slapped Jacques on the back, Jacques rose to his feet and stuck a finger threateningly in the guy's face.

Jacques is a jerk.

She got her feet securely beneath her. She felt the sudden acceleration of her heart. She took a moment to mentally pre-pared herself — and jumped.

Svetlana's feet hit the yard-wide top surface of the red brick wall. She touched down on the wall, her descent slowing be-fore her momentum pushed her forward, over the edge. She hit the ground with her feet properly spread, her knees bent. She made a smooth roll — the same one she had practiced so many times in parachute-training — and came up on one knee, her silenced Mauser in her right hand, searching for a target that was not to be found.

She adjusted the canvas bag over her shoulder, then moved forward swiftly, at a fast walk, not jogging, but not taking a leisurely stroll, either.

She found a downstairs window open. Svetlana moved away from the window. Time permitting, she'd make the in-vasion of the mansion and see what she could find. But first things first — she had to find out what was inside the big boat-house. That was where the serious expensive construction had been going on.

Svetlana passed the small tin shed where Browne and Rodney had been held captive. Sudden noise from inside the mansion caused Svetlana to freeze in her tracks. She held the Mauser securely in both hands, the silenced muzzle searching out the source of the sound. It was just the men inside the house, shouting once more over someone's very good fortune, or someone's very bad luck.

Svetlana moved on, passing silently from shadow to shadow, her feet making no more noise than an owl's wings through the night air.

She saw Arturo. He was sitting in a chair that was tipped back against the boathouse. For a moment Svetlana wondered whether he'd fallen asleep, because his chin was down near his chest, but then he looked upward, and his face glowed eerily in the moonlight. He turned his attention out to sea. The boathouse was so long that fully fifty feet of it stretched out into the water, with twenty feet of it anchored to solid ground. Even by the lavish standards of southern Florida, it was an enormous, opulent, over-built boathouse

The biggest trouble with the Sleeping Beauty dart was its short range. Hollow-point .32-caliber ammunition was murderous within forty yards; Sleeping Beauty had a maximum effective range of twenty yards — and not another inch beyond that, Burke had emphatically warned.

Thirty yards of open area separated Svetlana from the boathouse. The close-cropped lawn offered no shelter. Kneeling in shadows, Svetlana studied Arturo. He kept his gaze turned away from her and toward the water.

She couldn't take the time to use a longer but safer path the boathouse. The direct approach would have to do. Raising the Mauser to shoulder height and holding it in both hands in a modified Weaver stance, she stepped out of the shadows. Aiming at the sentry, she walked slowly, soundlessly.

Arturo must have sensed her presence more than anything else. He reached down to his left. Svetlana squeezed the trigger twice. The first Sleeping Beauty hit Arturo in the chest, the second one in the throat. He kicked just once before falling to the ground, knocking over the chair that he had been sitting in.

Svetlana hurried over. She touched Arturo's throat, felt for his pulse and found it. She looked beneath his chair. That was when Svetlana's blood went cold. What Arturo had been reaching for was a Czech-made Model 61 Skorpion submachine pistol. The tiny weapon was fitted with a silencer. It was the weapon of choice for many terrorist organizations around the world.

Svetlana put the chair upright again. She grabbed Arturo by the shoulders and hauled him into the chair, leaning him back so that it appeared as though he'd fallen asleep at his post with his head against the boathouse. She took the Skorpion and stuffed it into her canvas bag. The foot-long silencer stuck out through the flap.

The boathouse door facing the mansion was unlocked. Svetlana slipped through it. She waited a moment, her back to the door, her eyes open wide so they would adjust quickly to the almost nonexistent light. She reached into the canvas bag and found the miniature flashlight. With a touch of the button a beam of narrow-focused illumination shot from the metal instrument.

It wasn't simply a very large boathouse. The interior construction was completely different, long and narrow with heavily built walkways running the length of the structure on both sides. The wench-and-hoist system rigged to the rafters appeared to be enormously strong.

Svetlana walked deeper into the boathouse. There wasn't a

single tool that had not been properly put away after the day's work. Not a speck of grime or grease anywhere. There was a certain military ship-shape aura to the place that made a shiver work up Svetlana's spine. Wherever she looked, she saw the handiwork of military men who took orders, not civilian workers who received instructions.

Svetlana walked down the side ramp. She couldn't see into the water because of the darkness, but there appeared to be tracks, almost like railroad tracks, leading up from the water inside the boathouse. Guide runners for docking boats? Possibly, but the runners didn't seem like any that Svetlana had seen before, and she'd spent her fair share of time around boats.

The internal clock in Svetlana's head warned her that she'd spent enough time in the boathouse. The boat it had been built for was gone. Whatever vessel the boathouse had been made to house either hadn't been purchased yet, or was out to sea for the evening.

Svetlana went to the door, opened it just a crack, and listened carefully. Hearing nothing unusual, she stepped out into the dark night, the silenced Mauser pistol in her hand.

And that was when all hell broke loose.

CHAPTER NINE

Petyr had gotten down on one knee so he could look up into the face of Arturo, his unconscious comrade, who was slouched in the chair. Petyr had been grinning a moment earlier, thinking that Arturo had fallen asleep at his post. When Petyr slapped his friend lightly across the face to awaken him, Arturo slumped to the side, nearly falling out of his chair. That was when Petyr saw the small silver dart sticking in the side of Arturo's neck. He plucked out the dart — and then Svetlana stepped out of the boathouse door just five feet away.

Svetlana immediately raised her Mauser.

Petyr was a professional to the core. He lashed out with a lightning-swift side kick. The arch of his shoe caught Svetlana in the right wrist. The Mauser slipped from her numbed fingers.

It was, at that point, a battle between a hundred-twenty-five-pound woman and a two-hundred-pound man, each trained in self-defense and combat tactics.

Petyr recognized who his foe was immediately. His eyes widened, and he felt a suggestion of a smile tugged at the left corner of his mouth. He considered himself a match in combat to most any man, and in his heart knew that no woman was his equal. When Svetlana bent forward at the waist, her knees bent, he recognized the stance as a schooled one.

Neither combatant spoke a word. Svetlana's eyes were intense, bright in the moonlight. Petyr had never battled a woman before. Not a real fight. There was the woman he had raped in Kansas City who had fought valiantly, but she was a weak combatant and not much of a challenge for Petyr. After Petyr had killed her, he felt he'd been cheated, because the battle hadn't been worthy of his abilities.

He moved forward slowly, his two-hundred pounds carried smoothly on the balls of his feet. When Svetlana took a dancing step to her left, he watched the way her breasts bounced beneath the tight-fitting lightweight black sweater. His smile broadened, his lips pulling back around his teeth.

He saw the canvas bag at her hip, held there with a strap over her shoulder. When she took another retreating step from Petyr's advance, he saw something sticking up through the bag's flap. It took a moment for him to recognize the object as the silencer of Arturo's machine pistol.

Petyr faked a kick. When Svetlana reacted, putting a hand down in defense, he attacked with a straight right fist. The blow was aimed for Svetlana's nose. She ducked enough to take the punch to her head, just above the hairline. Though it was a glancing blow, the force of it dazed her. She raised her hands defensively as Petyr stepped closer.

Petyr's second attack was a side kick aimed for Svetlana's stomach. His legs were particularly powerful, and he knew that one solid kick to the solar plexus and the busty woman — no matter what her training and physical conditioning might be — would have the breath knocked out of her, and the fight would be over. He was confident of that.

Too confident, he discovered.

Svetlana gracefully sidestepped the kick, and as Petyr's foot stabbed harmlessly past her, she swung her left arm in a curving arc upward, catching his ankle and flipping his leg high over his head. Petyr hit the ground hard. He spun immediately into a defensive posture, his arms up high as he turned to face his adversary's counterattack.

Svetlana moved in for the rabbit punch to the back of

Petyr's head. Her short, chopping strike missed its target. All she managed was a glancing blow to his ear. The follow-through allowed Petyr to grab her wrist. While still on the ground, he spun on his hip and kicked upward. His foot connected savagely with Svetlana's ribs, just beneath her left breast. The breath gushed from her lungs, and she catapulted backward.

Don't give up! Petyr scrambled to his feet. The last thing in the world he wanted was for the stunning woman with the amazing body to suddenly give up the fight. What fun would be left for Petyr if she did that?

He watched as she rolled quickly and then rose to a standing position. She was trying to pretend that the kick hadn't hurt her, but Petyr could see into Svetlana's eyes, and he could tell that the pain in her ribs was intense.

Don't give up! Don't make it so easy it's no fun for me!

He could hear her breathing now, and the killer instinct in him whispered that he was the cat and she was his wounded mouse. He stepped in a bit too close. Svetlana snapped off a side kick that hit him on the hip and sent him staggering two steps backward. He smiled. There wasn't the power in her kick now that had been there seconds earlier.

Petyr stepped in again.

Svetlana faked another side kick, which Petyr reacted to, then she spun, turning her back to him. As he moved in, thinking she was about to run away, her right fist came around in a wide arc. The back of her fist, traveling with extraordinary velocity in its wide, lengthy swing, hit him solidly on the ear. His head whipped to the side and his knees bent. It sounded like a kettle drum was in his skull and being struck. The ringing in his head was deafening. Petyr was hurt, and he knew it.

"Bitch," he whispered, speaking Balkan-accented English.

He felt a trickle of blood dribbling down the side of his face from his cut ear. He blinked his eyes several times before he cleared his vision. He had a fight on his hands now. A real fight, just like he had wanted.

Svetlana danced a step backward. With her left hand, she adjusted the canvas bag properly on her hip, so that it would stay out of the way during the fight. For a couple seconds, her fingertips rested on the silencer, as though weighing the possibilities of getting the machine pistol out of the bag before Petyr could stop her.

Petyr's lips pulled back away from his teeth again. It wasn't a smile this time—more like the grimace of a snarling, wounded big cat. He moved in again, inviting Svetlana's attack.

She went for his eyes, shooting her left hand straight out, thumb searching for vulnerable eyeball. Petyr blocked the attack, countering with an immediate left hook to the ribs. His fist slammed into the voluptuous woman's body just above her hip. Once again, the breath left her lungs in a great gush. As she doubled over, Petyr went on the offensive, taking a half-step to his right and lashing out again, this time to the kidneys. Svetlana's head snapped back on her shoulders and her spine arched backward as she writhed in agony, dropping to her knees.

But Petyr wasn't finished with her yet. Not even close.

He used the edge of his hand to karate chop her on the back of the neck. Svetlana fell forward on the grass, her eyes barely open as she teetered on the edge of consciousness. She was completely helpless now, vulnerable to whatever the Russian wanted to do to her.

Petyr rolled Svetlana onto her back. He could see that she was groggy, but not unconscious. *Perfect! Now she'll know what's being done to her.*

He dropped down on her, sitting on Svetlana's pelvis. She raised a hand to defend herself. He batted her hand aside, chuckling as he did so.

"Stupid bitch!" he whispered again, speaking English so

that his victim knew exactly what he thought of her.

He put his hands over Svetlana's breasts and gouged his fingers deep into the plump mounds. Even though only semiconscious, Svetlana cried out in pain. Petyr slapped her across the face. He grabbed the black sweater between the mounds of her breasts, bunched the fabric in his fists, and pulled apart with all his might. The sweater rent in half from the neckline down to Svetlana's stomach. An instant later, Petyr ripped the brassiere in half, tearing it between the lacy cups to reveal the pale orbs of Svetlana's bountiful bosom.

Svetlana raised her hands again, her fingers curled, clawing at Petyr's face. He defended himself without fear, catching her wrists and pinning her arms to her sides with his knees. He slapped her left breast savagely and watched the mounds jiggle tautly. He laughed. It was the excited yelp of a hyena at last confident of making a kill.

As Svetlana wiggled beneath him, trying to buck him off her body, Petyr contemplated punching her in the face. He decided that she was far too beautiful to damage in such a way. Perhaps later he'd allow himself the pleasure of feeling her nose smash beneath his fist. For now, he wanted her to remain beautiful.

Petyr pushed himself backward, so that he was sitting on Svetlana's thighs. As she started to attack him once more, he slashed down with a right fist that smashed into her unprotected stomach. As Svetlana, unable to breathe, writhed in agony on the grass, Petyr worked quickly. First he pulled the canvas bag from her and tossed it aside. His hands were trembling with anticipation as he fumbled with her black jeans, unfastening the brass snap at her stomach. The instant he had her zipper down, he grabbed the waistband of her jeans and pulled the garment down her legs with all his might.

The jeans came off completely. Svetlana's shoes were ripped from her feet. Petyr got to his feet, laughing openly now, holding the black jeans in his right hand as he looked down at his victim. She was stunningly beautiful, her sweater torn in half to expose her breasts, her pale legs shining in the moonlight as she struggled to get her knees beneath her. She still wore her panties, and Petyr was glad she did. It would be one more article of clothing that he could tear from her body, one more act of defilement he could administer before he felt the sweet ecstasy of his own hard flesh spearing into her.

Petyr's laughter had at last drawn the attention of his comrades inside the mansion. He was angry that soon he would have to share his conquest with the others—but the sharing would wait until he was finished with her.

"Come on, little bitch, don't stop fighting," Petyr taunted.

His hooded eyes were glazed as he watched the woman's breasts swaying. He held her jeans by the legs. The jeans weighed more than he expected. She had things in the pockets, he realized. He wasn't worried. The woman on her knees could hardly breathe. Petyr wondered if, when he pumped his lust-hardened flesh into her body, he'd feel the heat of her breath against his face. It was a tempting question to ponder.

"You're mine, little bitch."

He slapped her with her jeans. She tried to defend herself, but there was very little strength left in her, it seemed. Amusement bubbled up out of Petyr's chest. He swung the jeans at her again, whipping her with her own clothes.

Svetlana caught the jeans and held onto them. When Petyr pulled at the garment, intending upon ripping them from her grasp, he pulled Svetlana so that she rose up onto one knee. For several seconds, Petyr looked into Svetlana's eyes. He was enjoying the tug of war. He saw her right hand come out of the rear pocket of the black denim slacks. There was something in that small hand.

Awareness dawned on Petyr a split second before he saw the pencil of red flame leap from the muzzle, and heard the tiny black weapon scream its rage.

The .25-caliber Junior Colt was not loaded with knock-out darts. It was loaded with Remington-made semi-jacketed hollow-points. The first round that Svetlana fired hit Petyr in the cheek. His head snapped back from the impact. His eyes registered the confusion that was going through his brain. When Svetlana fired a second time, putting this round into his chest, Petyr looked down at the spreading red stain on his shirt. He was still looking down at his chest as he toppled backward and his body hit the ground. He died with his eyes open, his brain unable to quite comprehend just exactly what went wrong with a fight that he'd felt was so completely under control.

Svetlana, wearing only her panties and the tattered remains of her sweater and brassiere, rushed to the canvas bag where the Skorpion waited with lethal anticipation. Behind her, from the mansion, she heard the worried shouts of *comrades* speaking Russian as they called out to their brother soldier-in-arms who had made the fatal mistake of underestimating Svetlana's skills.

Katrina had never before seen darkness quite so complete. She was one hundred feet beneath the surface of the water at midnight. The only light was the dull green glow of her instrument panel. Behind her, Juanita sat quietly, knowing that she was to remain silent. Katrina could feel the young woman's fear, but she could also sense confidence. Juanita trusted Katrina with her life. She would jump off a cliff without questioning why if Katrina asked her to.

A soft smile touched Katrina's lips. *If only every soldier in my command was so loyal and trusting.*

The radar screen informed Katrina that she was within fifty

yards of the cocaine shipment. There was an urge to turn on the electric lights, but Katrina tamped down the desire. Turning on the lights was an enormous expenditure of battery power. When she was on top of the shipment, she'd turn on the lights, and then do it only long enough to attach the towing cables. Then she'd switch the lights off again and follow her sonar readings to get back to her seaside mansion and the newly constructed boathouse that kept her mini submarine a secret from prying eyes.

Katrina turned her face slightly to the side and asked, "How are you doing?"

"Very well, Comrade Luvesky," Juanita replied. There was a grateful quality to her tone, as though the simple act of breaking the silence had given her enormous relief.

"Everything is going according to plan. We'll make the pickup inside ten minutes. We'll be on our way back to the base before you know it. There will be a wonderful celebration tonight, comrade. A private celebration. Would you like that?"

"Yes, Comrade Luvesky. Of course."

But Katrina's thoughts shifted from the petite brunette with the tantalizing desire to please to a buxom woman with the devilish ability to avoid seduction.

Stop thinking about Svetlana! Vlad will have her at the base when you return. Think about the shipment now. There's time enough to seduce that frightened little capitalist tart when you get her into your bedroom.

The green-glowing sonar screen began beeping softly in double-time. That meant she was within twenty-five yards of the homing beacon inside the cocaine shipment. Katrina's heart beat more quickly. She cut the power to the propeller and drifted forward, her speed slowing. The beeping increased in frequency, then turned into a constant buzz. Katrina switched off the audio signal.

"It should be right in front of us," Katrina said as she

reached for the toggle switch on the control panel that activated the floodlights.

She turned the toggle upward. Four floodlights, two on each side of the submarine, came to life. Directly in front of her was the coffin-like plastic box containing nearly pure cocaine. For several seconds, Katrina simply looked at the box, amazed at how perfect the plan was that she and Mr. Bigg had devised so long ago.

Juanita, twisting around in her rearward-facing seat, looked over Katrina shoulder and whispered, "Amazing, Comrade Luvesky! You couldn't have found it more easily!"

"Back in your position, Juanita," Katrina replied, not entirely ignoring the flattery.

She flipped up another silver toggle on the control panel. Two small, hissing explosions sounded on the plastic box. Four waterproof canvas bags about the size of basketballs, attached to each corner of the container, inflated with air. Between two of the balls, in front and in back, was a heavy towing cable.

"Ready for your part?" Katrina asked.

"Of course, Comrade Luvesky."

Katrina turned the submarine around slowly. She didn't want the propeller to kick up any silt from the ocean floor. Visibility, at this vulnerable stage of the operation, was absolutely critical. When the submarine was facing directly away from the cocaine shipment, Katrina cut the electrical power to the forward floodlights, then turned on the power to the rear lights.

She twisted in the captain's seat to look over Juanita's shoulder.

The petite Mexican said in a coolly professional voice, "Activating towing arm."

A single metal arm unfolded from the rear of the submarine. Attached to the end of the arm was a metal clamp. The arm was operated by controls at Juanita's right elbow. With practiced ease, Juanita reached out with the mechanical arm and brought the hand clamp to the towing cable held off the floor of the ocean by two of the four canvas balloons. She locked the clamp into place around the towing cable.

"The package is secure, Comrade Luvesky."

Katrina left the floodlights on as she transferred power to the propeller. Silt and dirt were kicked up off the ocean floor, swirling around in the inky water. Katrina could feel the submarine struggling with the additional burden. Then, as she watched the container come free from its resting place on the ocean floor, she felt the submarine pick up speed.

She switched off the lights and angled the underwater vessel upward so that she could pull the container through the water without obstructions.

"We'll be home soon," Katrina said, forcing her tone to remain calm even though her heart was beating triumphantly. "When the submarine has been put away and everything is in order, then we can celebrate."

"Yes, Comrade Luvesky." After a moment, Juanita added, "It is my honor to please you."

Svetlana heard men coming out of the mansion, but she didn't dare look that way. Her time was running out. She picked up her silenced Mauser and stuffed it into the canvas backpack, then put in the Junior Colt, which had saved her life, as well. She pulled out the silenced Skorpion and thumbed off the safety.

Svetlana slipped her head and arm into the backpack strap. She felt the coarse canvas material rub against her breasts. She looked down for only an instant and was shocked to see her own breasts were completely naked, the white cups of her brassiere flopping helplessly to the sides of her body, her sweater torn in half. Beneath that, she had on panties and nothing else. Her shoes and socks had come off when the soldier had ripped her jeans down her legs.

An authoritative order, hissed in guttural Russian, drew Svetlana's attention. She looked up just in time to see Jacques ordering another man to rush around to his right. Svetlana raised the Skorpion and squeezed the trigger. The fully automatic machine pistol bucked in her hand, spitting out lead at an incredibly high rate. The weapon's roar was diminished to a deep rumbling sound because of the long, effective silencer.

Svetlana recognized her target — it was Deiter — just before he cartwheeled under the impact of the slugs hitting him. The wall behind him dripped with blood.

She heard the *brrrrup* of a weapon identical to her own. A bullet hit her canvas bag, ricocheting off one of the grenades inside. Svetlana started running. She was caught out in the open, but she moved fast to her right, running parallel to the mansion. As more men began streaming out the rear door, she sent them a spray of lead, sweeping the area quickly at waist-level. Two men went down hard and screamed in agony.

Every soldier knows there is nothing worse than getting gut-shot. Seeing their comrades cut down in such a fashion caused several more soldiers to pull up short. A stationary target is easy to hit, and the soldiers should have known that. Svetlana dropped two of them with three-shot bursts delivered with pinpoint accuracy.

Svetlana had just slipped behind a tree when she heard the *thud* of a bullet slamming into the thick trunk. She wheeled to face her attacker and squeezed the trigger of her confiscated Skorpion. The weapon bucked twice in her hands, then was silent as the slide locked open on an empty magazine. The soldier who had stepped out of the shadows and had very nearly ambushed her fell backward, his arms outstretched in death.

Svetlana tossed her Skorpion aside and grabbed her latest

victim's weapon. How many more soldiers were there? She guessed that not many men had seen her, judging from the way they were shouting to each other to go this way and that way. Her Russian was excellent and she recognized that soldiers were asking where *they* were, which meant Katrina's soldiers thought there was more than one attacker. In the back of her mind she wished she'd taken the time to pick up her jeans and shoes. Was there enough left behind to incriminate her? She didn't know. All she was certain of was that this operation had gone terribly, terribly wrong, and with each passing second, the likelihood of her escaping Katrina Luvesky's compound became worse.

Another soldier moved around the side of the mansion. He took a look at Svetlana and raised his weapon, though he did not fire. He apparently wasn't expecting to see a voluptuous beauty standing in shadows, her breasts quivering in the moonlight. His appreciation of feminine beauty was his undoing. Svetlana put a three-round burst into him from his navel to his chest.

The front gates were fifty yards away. Svetlana now saw that as her most likely avenue of escape. She reached into her canvas bag and extracted a "flash-bang" grenade. She pulled the pin and gave the grenade a toss in the direction of harried shouts she had heard earlier. Squeezing her eyes tightly shut, she got down on one knee and waited, plugging her ears with her fingers. Men were shouting, and one screamed that he could see him and that he looked wounded.

Then the grenade went off with deafening sound and blinding light. Only after the explosion had ended did Svetlana open her eyes and unplug her ears.

Four men were in the clearing where she'd tossed the grenade. After the explosion, all four were standing, but they were staggering now, disoriented by the noise of the blast, blinded by the brilliance of the light it emitted. Calmly, knowing exactly what she had to do, Svetlana put the four men down with devastating three-shot bursts. When the men hit the thick lawn, they did not even twitch.

Svetlana was very nearly at the front gate when Jacques stepped out of the shadows. He held a Skorpion in each hand. The look on his face was utterly demonic as he moved out of the shadows. He could have shot Svetlana from ambush, but he seemed to want Svetlana to see him before he killed her.

Jacques sent two savage streams of lead at Svetlana, firing wildly, chewing up the ground around her as he tried to track her movement.

She sent four bullets into his chest.

Svetlana ran barefooted through the front gates of the compound, her mind in a whirl. Would the police be showing up soon? The only real noise that had been created throughout the firefight was when she had used her little Junior Colt, and from the flash-bang grenade. Other than that, all the weapons had been equipped with silencers.

She jogged on, unmindful of her own nudity, aware of every noise, every movement in shadows, as she moved farther and farther away from the carnage she had created.

Katrina knew something was wrong even before she smoothly guided the mini submarine onto the docking hoist. Her sixth sense was warning her in that special way she couldn't describe. As she waited in four feet of water for Petyr to winch up the hoist and raise the submarine into the boathouse, she became more and more convinced that the operation she had felt was going flawlessly was somehow in jeopardy.

After waiting a full two minutes for someone to begin hoisting the submarine up into the loading dock, Katrina snapped angrily, "Get out there and find out what's happened!"

"Yes, Comrade Luvesky," Juanita replied quickly.

Katrina remained focused on her instrument panel as she heard the lower hatch door being opened. Katrina watched as Juanita, now in the water, swam in front of the submarine and hauled her slender body onto the hoist.

There'd better be a damned good reason for this, Katrina thought bitterly as she began contemplating the punishments she would give to her men for not manning their posts as she had ordered them to.

Juanita disappeared, pulling herself up out of the water. Several seconds later, Katrina heard the powerful electric motors come to life as the heavy mini submarine was slowly lifted out of the water.

Katrina could hardly believe the carnage she had come home to. Everyone was dead. Everyone except Arturo. He was sleeping. No, not exactly sleeping — drugged. Svetlana had slapped him and slapped him until his eyes finally opened, and even then he could hardly talk.

Katrina found dead men — her soldiers, who she had thought were well-trained — strewn everywhere. It was as though someone had thrown an orgy, and everyone had discarded their clothes throughout the compound . . .except that they'd left dead bodies inside those clothes.

Who could have done such a thing? Were the police on their way? Katrina had already outwitted the authorities once, but it wouldn't be so easy to outwit them when she had nearly pure cocaine still attached to the towing arm of her mini-submarine which, thank goodness, the American law enforcement agencies hadn't seen during their first raid on the premises.

Katrina and Juanita had been on land less than five minutes

when Vlad arrived. He saw Jacques's corpse, but showed no outward sign of emotion upon discovering that his comrade was dead.

"Is Svetlana with you?" Katrina asked.

Vlad shook his head.

"She wasn't in her motel room?"

Again, the Russian giant shook his head.

Katrina turned to Juanita. "I want you to find her. Bring her here. Don't accept *no* for an answer. Is that clear?"

"Yes, Comrade Luvesky."

Juanita, still in wet clothes, hurried off to do her mistress's bidding.

Katrina turned to Vlad and said in her most commanding tone, "I need you tonight, Vlad. There's been a terrible accident. The only one remaining here who has not been killed in Arturo. I want you to take the other bodies, weight them down, and distribute them in the sea. Be careful. Don't let anyone see what you're doing. I need the bodies where they'll be eaten by the fish and never seen again. Do I make myself clear?"

Vlad nodded.

"Good. Then hurry back. These are terrible times, Vlad. We have an enemy, and until I find out who that enemy is, none of us can have a moment's rest."

As Katrina watched her dutiful giant gathering the corpses — carrying the bodies as though they hardly weighed anything at all — she wondered who might have conducted the attack upon her residence. She immediately ruled out the legal law enforcement authorities of the United States. They were too bound by rules and regulations to do something like this. Besides, she had given those agencies a terrible black eye after the first raid when they had found nothing at all incriminating — thanks in part to Svetlana's forewarning, Katrina reminded herself — so it was highly unlikely that they would be trying anything against her again soon.

But someone had obviously not been intimidated. Someone had come right into her own camp and killed every one of her on-site soldiers, with the singular exception of one man who appeared to be thoroughly drugged up and unlikely to provide much information on what had happened, if he could provide any information at all.

So what the hell was going on? Was this the work of a rival drug gang? The American Mafia? Freelancers from Columbia or Mexico, perhaps?

None of it made any sense to Katrina, but she could not deny its reality, because Vlad continued walking past her, carrying one bloody corpse after another, tossing the dead bodies into a boat.

Everything had seemed to be going so perfectly with the operation. Too perfectly, Katrina now knew.

Several hours later, alone in her bedroom, Katrina made a decision on who she would call. Rutgar. He was a German, deadly as a stiletto switchblade, and he had his own crew of men who were loyal to him. In the past, Katrina had kept Rutgar and his men at a distance, allowing them to operate the Moscow Cartel's Mediterranean contraband weapons operation. Rutgar's men were battle-hardened mercenaries who knew what was expected of them and would kill without asking questions.

If she made the call, she could have Rutgar and his men at her Florida headquarters within forty-eight hours. Not quite enough time to be there when the first full shipment of cocaine was to be transferred to Alberto Sacci, but soon after that.

It was only as Katrina began feeling a sense that the worst was behind her that she finally understood exactly how shaken she had been from the attack upon her headquarters. Would Rutgar and his men be enough, or should she call in another unit?

Katrina quickly discarded that notion. It was always a dangerous proposition to start mixing units. Power vacuums tended to form whenever one squad of soldiers began mingling with another. Katrina wasn't in any mood to deal with such trivialities as whose responsibility it was to do which small but critically important chore.

Burke listened to Svetlana's recorded audio transmission three times. He felt relieved, even though such emotions could not possibly bring his old friend, Sir Malcomb Sitwell, back to life. The message was:

"Sir Malcomb Sitwell was murdered, as well as family and domestic help. I believe I'm on the trail of the killer, and will see that justice is served. Next transmission uncertain. Dig up any information you have on Katrina Luvesky, probably a Russian national. Any links to Russian intelligence? Russian organized crime? She's got money and clout, and she's savage as hell when she thinks she's cornered. Over and out."

Svetlana had called on the secure line that only Burke knew about. The calls were never answered and immediately went into recording.

Burke rose to his feet and crossed the room to the old battered metal filing cabinet. He opened the top drawer and in the far corner of it found the half-pint bottle of Jack Daniel's whiskey. He unscrewed the cap and raised the bottle.

"To you, Sir Malcomb," he said aloud. "You were honorable to the very end. I never believed you committed suicide. I never believed you killed your family. You were too good of a man to do something like that. So rest in peace, my friend. Whoever is responsible for what happened to you will pay.

That's my promise to you."

He took another sip, then a third, then recapped the bottle and tucked it back in among the file folders.

It really was true. Sir Malcomb Sitwell was too good of a man to have committed a horrific murder-slash-suicide.

Now was time to find out who *had* killed him.

Katrina was dressed in another one of her mannish dark suits. She wore black trousers with a white starched shirt and a narrow, black silk necktie. An exquisitely tailored suit coat completed the outfit. Only her shoes, black pumps with stiletto heels, were distinctly feminine.

Katrina liked the way the clothes made her appear. She knew that she was a woman. No doubt there. But she liked to appear strong, tough—mannish, even. That way, men treated her with more respect than they otherwise might. Especially when she towered over them in height.

"Will you be taking a weapon, Comrade Luvesky?" Juanita asked.

Katrina shook her head. "No need. Alberto Sacci has as much to gain by this partnership as the Moscow Cartel does. He's not going to do anything foolish at this critical juncture. Besides, I'll have Vlad with me. What more protection do I need?"

"I could go along."

Katrina looked in the mirror at Juanita. She knew that Juanita didn't like the security arrangements that had been made for the first transfer of drugs with Alberto Sacci. That was fine. Katrina didn't like them herself. But until she had Rutgar and his men safely ensconced within the walls of the Moscow Cartel's Florida headquarters, Katrina would have to live with the fact that she was dangerously understaffed.

"Have Vlad bring the car around," Katrina said in a

commanding voice. "Juanita, I want you to have Svetlana here when I return. Do I make myself clear?"

"Yes, Comrade Luvesky."

"She's slippery. Very slippery. See that she doesn't get away. Persuade her that she must come. Understood?"

"Yes, Comrade Luvesky. I understand completely."

Alberto Sacci could hardly believe his eyes. Was the tall Russian woman really in the back seat of the delivery car? What balls. What unbelievable balls. Never in a thousand years would Alberto ride in a car with that much pure cocaine in the trunk, but that's exactly what Katrina Luvesky was doing.

"You believe that, boss?" Tomas asked. He was Sacci's number one bodyguard.

"I see it," Sacci replied, "but I don't believe it."

"Come on, boss, let's get inside. I don't want you being seen when she gets outta the car."

"Yeah, Tomas. Good idea."

Alberto Sacci turned away from the nightclub's parking lot and stepped into the chaos inside.

The nightclub catered to a crowd that was mostly in its twenties, and the music was loud and discordant. Sacci didn't care. The blaring music made it absolutely impossible for any conversation to be recorded. Furthermore, with the continual hustle and bustle of the nightclub going on, nobody would notice that one person drove a certain nondescript sedan into the parking lot, while a different person drove that same nondescript sedan out of the parking lot an hour later.

An hour earlier, Sacci had sent three of his men to get a corner booth. He kept the men there, having them order round after round of drinks even though they weren't allowed to swallow a drop. When Sacci approached the booth, his bodyguards hurried out of the way.

Sacci put his lips close to Tomas's ear, but still had to shout to be heard. "See to it that the lady ain't pushed around when she's going through the crowd. I don't want nobody gettin' grab-ass with her."

"You got it, boss." Tomas promised.

Sacci slid into the booth, folded his hands, and waited as patiently as a fundamentally impatient man could wait. When he finally saw Katrina making her way through the crowd — and she was not hard to spot, immaculately dressed in a man's dark suit, and standing well over six feet tall in her high-heels — Sacci felt a sudden surge of confidence go through him. He couldn't say why it was so, but working with Katrina Luvesky made him feel secure that all his plans and dreams were about to become a reality.

"Slide on in," Sacci said, half-rising from his booth bench.

In the middle of the table were a set of car keys. There were only two keys on the ring. As Katrina sat down, she nonchalantly placed another key ring on the table. Her ring contained just two keys as well.

"This is a nice setup."

In order for Sacci to hear her, Katrina had to lean close and put her mouth near his ear. When she did, he caught a whiff of her perfume. The scent reminded him that though she wore a mannishly tailored suit, she was definitely a woman — a very feminine woman at that.

"Noise like this makes is pretty damned hard to record over."

Katrina nodded. "Smart. Very smart. I like that in a business partner."

Sacci thought of putting his hand on Katrina's leg beneath the table. The thought didn't last long. Finding beautiful women to have sex with was easy — finding someone who could deliver nearly pure cocaine on a weekly basis was not.

"It's in the trunk?" he asked.

Katrina nodded.

"Ready to let the boys take a look?"

Again, Katrina nodded.

Sacci looked into her eyes, then asked the question that had been eating a hole in his stomach since he saw her in the parking lot. "Why risk being in the car with the stuff? Ain't you got people to handle that for you?"

"Of course I do. But why? This is a secure operation. You're a professional, and so am I. You know what's expected of you, and I know what's expected of me. I rode in the car because, at least during the initial stages of a partnership, I like taking a hands-on approach. Maybe that seems dangerous, but as far as I'm concerned, it's more dangerous to be so far removed from the operation that you risk losing focus, perspective, and control." She turned the full force of her sea blue eyes upon Sacci. "Do you understand what I mean?"

For the first time in his adult life, Sacci was speechless. After several seconds of silence, he finally nodded. Never in his long and illustrious life had he ever gone into business with anyone like Katrina Luvesky, and if Mr. Bigg was half as competent as she was, then there wasn't any doubt in his heart that he'd be a billionaire before three years had passed.

When Sacci finally found his voice, he asked, "Can I buy you a drink?"

Katrina again shook her head. "Let's have our men take a drive and inspect the merchandise."

Sacci made an almost imperceptible move with his right hand. Instantly, Tomas hurried forward. He snatched both sets of key rings from the center of the table, and upon turning, handed one to Vlad.

"I'm worried about that man of yours," Sacci said, his lips close to Katrina's ear. "It's not that he's not a good man. I'd hate like hell to have to go against him. But he's so damned big he draws attention."

"You're right," Katrina replied. "From now on, I'll leave him back and use different men. It's not like he's the only muscle Mr. Bigg's got on the payroll."

Twenty minutes passed before Vlad and Tomas returned to the nightclub. When they did, Tomas was smiling. Vlad had his usual stony expression, though when his gaze met Katrina's, the giant nodded his head.

Katrina turned to Sacci and put her lips close enough to his ear that he could feel the warmth of her breath when she spoke. "It looks like we're going to have a long and profitable partnership, Mr. Sacci. I'll see you again next week."

Before Alberto Sacci could say a word, Katrina slipped out of the booth. The cars with the money and the cocaine would be driven by soldiers. Should they get arrested, their families would be taken care of. Katrina and Sacci would return to their respective residences in different vehicles, neither one even remotely capable of being implicated in the illegal transaction that had just taken place.

Juanita pulled the shiny red Lincoln Navigator into the parking lot and turned off the ignition. The motel was laid out in an L-shaped design, and from where she had parked, she could see every door. It was not an expensive motel. In fact, it was a rather cheap one, considering the standards of Key West. Some of the locals, Juanita had learned, had called the motel a "passion pit" because secret lovers of every age — and often of the same gender — used the motel for afternoon trysts.

She reached into the small clutch purse she had on the passenger side seat. Inside the purse was an electronic stun gun. Two small metal rods protruded from the top of the instrument. It was simple to operate — just touch those two rods to a person's body and depress the trigger. The electrical charge more often than not rendered the victim incapable of walking for a full three minutes.

Juanita was hoping she would have the chance to demonstrate the weapon's non-lethal effectiveness upon Svetlana Simonov. She wanted to watch the voluptuous American woman drop to her knees when she was shocked with the electricity. Then Juanita would wrap all that luxurious blonde hair around her fist and drag the woman to the Navigator.

Memories of what Juanita had so recently seen flashed across the surface of her mind. When she had discovered the electronic eavesdropping devices in the mansion, Juanita had gone immediately to warn her mistress, Comrade Katrina Luvesky, about the breach in security. But when she rounded the hallway corner, Juanita found herself face to face with Svetlana and Katrina. Katrina had Svetlana's wrists pinned to the wall, and at that very moment, she was sucking upon Svetlana's bountiful breasts through a sheer silk nightgown. It didn't matter to Juanita that Svetlana was clearly trying to avoid Katrina's seduction. All that mattered to Juanita was that she was suddenly no longer the one Katrina looked to when she wanted lesbian entertainment . . . and that was a condition that Juanita Diego was not willing to accept. Not without a fight.

She carried the stun gun in her right hand as she crossed the parking lot slowly. It was nearly midnight, and she heard people all around her. The laughter of people who had drunk too much offended the sense of discipline that Juanita held sacred. In the back of her mind she imagined the pleasure that would be hers when she watched the United States being brought to its knees.

The American capitalist bitch was registered in room twelve. Vlad had previously been sent to retrieve Svetlana Simonov, and it was only the fact that Comrade Luvesky had returned to a headquarters strewn with corpses that allowed Vlad to get away without punishment. It was the giant's absence from the compound that granted him the excuse to continue living.

From her left, Juanita heard a young couple laughing, or perhaps crying. Both were obviously quite inebriated. They were in the room two doors down from Svetlana's. Juanita hoped that they wouldn't give her any problem. If they did, then she'd kill them both. Juanita Diego considered all Americans with the same regard that she viewed disease-carrying rats, and killing them, she believed, was an act of kindness for the world.

Juanita stepped up to the door and paused a moment. She listened, but there was no sound of anyone inside the room. She glanced at her wristwatch. It was midnight. At that very moment, Comrade Luvesky was probably finalizing plans to exchange cocaine for American currency, Juanita knew.

She reached out with her left and, while still holding the electric stun-gun in her right hand, rapped on the door. A moment later she heard the rustling of bedcovers and the shuffling of feet.

"Who is it?"

Juanita recognized Svetlana's voice, and the sound of it grated on her nerves. Svetlana sounded groggy, slightly disoriented.

"I'm here on behalf of Katrina Luvesky," Juanita said, keeping her voice low enough so that it wouldn't carry far. "Please open the door. There's something important I must tell you."

"Who else is with you?"

Juanita didn't like the question on principle. "No one. Please open the door. There's something important I must say to you."

Juanita heard the scrape of a chain being removed from the lock. The door opened just a couple inches. Juanita put her hand on the door and, with what little weight she did have, pushed the door open wide.

Svetlana Simonov was forced several steps backward. She stood with green eyes wide with surprise, wearing nothing but matching lacy black brassiere and bikini panties. In her right hand was a lowball glass, and inside it was gin—and if Juanita's guess was correct, it was straight gin, and not the first one of the evening, either.

"Katrina Luvesky wishes to extend an invitation," Juanita said as she stepped into the room, pushing past the barrier of Svetlana's outstretched arm. "She would like you to be her guest. She wishes you to come immediately."

The smell of gin, like that of pine needles, filled the small motel room. Juanita suspected that more than one cocktail had been spilled. This pleased her. It meant the American whore was weak-willed . . . just as Juanita had suspected she would be.

"Well, you'll just have to tell Katrina that I can't make it. I've made other plans."

"Change them."

"I-I-I don't know if I can," Svetlana stammered.

Svetlana took a step backward, hit the foot of her bed, and sat clumsily upon the mattress. Juanita watched Svetlana's heavy breasts bouncing and felt a strange flush of desire go through her veins. She understood why Katrina might hunger for Svetlana. She was classically beautiful in all the right ways. She would be interesting . . . at least temporarily, Juanita decided.

"Are you drunk?"

"No," Svetlana answered. After a moment she amended, "Well, only a little."

"You're coming to headq—" Juanita snapped, then stopped herself.

She had nearly said "headquarters," and that would have been a breach of security that Comrade Luvesky would not appreciate. Juanita stepped closer to Svetlana, who remained seated on the bed. Juanita held up the electric stun-gun so that Svetlana could see it, then depressed the activator. Electrical current, blue and orange in color, arced from the tip of one metal rod to the other. Svetlana's eyes widened in fear, and she recoiled.

"You're coming with me," Juanita declared quietly, the undercurrent of violence evident in every word she spoke. "Make it easy on yourself. You're in no condition to fight me. You'll only get yourself hurt, and for no good reason at all."

"Okay, okay," Svetlana said. She raised her hands in defeat, and when she did, the gin sloshed out of her glass and onto her bosom and bra. She set the glass on the cheap carpet, then licked gin from her forefinger. "Just let me put something on and get packed and I'll be with you."

"There's no time for that."

"I'm not going there wearing just this!"

Juanita activated the stun-gun again, and when the electricity arced between the rod, Svetlana shrank away in horror.

"Okay! Okay!" she said, nearly shouting. She pushed herself off the bed and went to the small dressing table where her battered leather suitcase was. "This'll only take me a second." she said as she began tossing clothes into the suitcase.

"We're leaving now! Any more delays, and you get this!"

Juanita held the stun-gun close to Svetlana's face and activated it. The crackling electrical current made the voluptuous woman cry out in fear. Svetlana grabbed the two halves of her suitcase and squeezed the luggage closed, though she did not have the time to pull the zipper or fasten the locks properly. She had put less than half of her clothes in the luggage before Juanita had stopped her.

"Okay, you win," Svetlana said, her words slurred.

She held the suitcase under her right arm, pinned against her side to keep it from opening completely and spilling her clothes out. Barefooted, wearing only her brassiere and bikini panties, Svetlana stepped out into the motel parking lot, allowing Juanita to lead her to the big red Lincoln Navigator.

What Juanita did not notice was that though Svetlana's words were slurred, her jewel-like eyes were clear and bright, and though her suitcase had appeared completely empty before clothes had been tossed inside, in the secret compartment at the base of it were Svetlana's two favorite pistols, along with a very efficient titanium silencer.

CHAPTER TEN

Svetlana was fresh from the shower, back in the guest bed-room she'd occupied before — the room that was, not coin-cidentally, just down the hall from Katrina Luvesky's bed-room. The gin that Svetlana had on herself, and splashed lib-erally around the motel room, had completely fooled Juanita. When Svetlana was shown to her room, Juanita had de-manded, in icy tones, that she take a cold shower to *sober up before Comrade Luvesky returns.*

The only surprise for Svetlana was that it had been Juanita who had come to get her. Svetlana had figured Katrina would assign Vlad for the task. What could be more intimidating than having the mute Russian giant at the door? Instead, it was little Juanita, with her beautiful, hate-filled eyes and that silly stun-gun that would have been such poor defense against Svetlana's .32-caliber Mauser.

Juanita had let her defenses down several times, enough to give Svetlana information she probably was not intended to have. Katrina was a Russian, but whether she was a com-munist or not wasn't clear. Juanita was most definitely a Marxist, Svetlana decided, as confirmed by her use of the *comrade* title. What Svetlana had not yet learned was how these people had made it appear that Sir Malcomb Sitwell had mur-dered his family before committing suicide. Until she had that answer — and had made sure that the people responsible suf-fered grievously for their murderous actions — she wasn't go-ing to consider the assignment complete. Burke wouldn't want it any other way, and neither would his personally trained field operative, Svetlana Simonov.

The bedroom door opened. Juanita stepped halfway into the room.

"Don't you ever knock before entering?" Svetlana asked, holding a towel up to hide her nudity.

"Do your makeup," Juanita ordered. "Comrade Luvesky will return within the hour. I'll find something suitable for you to wear."

Juanita stepped out and closed the door. Svetlana smiled to herself. Juanita was jealous, she could tell. Perhaps it would be possible to divide the loyalties of the people surrounding Katrina, and by doing so, weaken their collective strength. It was a slim possibility, but still . . .

Sooner or later, Svetlana would find a loose string or two, and when she did, she would unravel the web of Katrina Luvesky's power.

When Katrina returned to the mansion, carrying the large suitcase stuffed with neatly bound American hundred-dollar bills, she listened carefully to every word that Juanita said. In the short time that Katrina had been away from the mansion in order to deliver the first shipment of cocaine to Alberto Sacci, much had happened. Rutgar and his men had boarded an Airbus and would be arriving at the mansion soon, perhaps as early as four o'clock in the morning. That was a full day sooner than Katrina's most optimistic estimation.

Katrina looked at her wristwatch. It was just a few minutes past three AM.

"And Svetlana is here?"

"Yes, Comrade Luvesky. She was at the motel. She'd been drinking."

Katrina's eyes narrowed as she looked down at Juanita. "Was she alone?"

"At the time, yes. I can't say whether she was alone earlier."

"How is she now?"

"She has taken a shower and appears better. I found some clothes for her to wear. I don't believe she's quite dressed yet."

Katrina nodded thoughtfully and patted the girl's cheek lightly. "Very good, Juanita. I've always been impressed with your thoughtfulness and efficiency. When the American is dressed, I want to see her. But not until she's looking her best."

"Yes, Comrade Luvesky."

"I had hoped to celebrate tonight, but it doesn't look like I'll be able to. Not properly. Not with Rutgar and his men arriving within the hour." Katrina sighed, the burden of responsibility occasionally weighing heavily upon her shoulders. "Business before pleasure, I suppose."

"Yes, Comrade Luvesky. Always."

Thirty minutes later, Katrina was sitting on the leather sofa in the library, and her once-happy mood was transforming into one of slowly-building anger. What was taking Svetlana so long?

Katrina sensed more than heard Vlad enter the room. For an enormously large man, he moved with a lightness of foot that Katrina found at times to be quite eerie.

"Yes, Vlad?"

He raised his hand, pointing out of the library.

"Svetlana?"

He shook his head, and then crooked a finger as though shooting a pistol.

"Rutgar and his men?"

Vlad nodded.

"Thank you. Show them in," Katrina said. Even as she mentally prepared herself for her meeting with Rutgar,

Katrina was contemplating what punishment she would mete out to her elusive and oh-so-tempting houseguest.

Rutgar stepped into the library, leading his eight hand-picked men. When Katrina saw him, she did not smile, though she felt confidence flow through her veins. Someone had attacked her headquarters and killed her men. Thank goodness she had been in the mini submarine at the time of the attack, or she might have been killed herself. But whoever the assailants had been, they wouldn't be so successful if they tried another attack. Not with Rutgar and his band of cut-throats within the high, three-feet-thick brick walls of the compound. Rutgar's killers were second to none.

"Thank you for coming so quickly," Katrina said, crossing the room with her long-legged stride. "I can assure you, Mr. Bigg will hear about your promptness and loyalty."

"Thank you, Comrade Luvesky," Rutgar replied.

"I'm sure it has been a tiring journey. Perhaps your men would like something to eat and drink while you and I discuss necessities." Katrina snapped her fingers. "Vlad, see to it that Rutgar's men have whatever they want." She snapped her fingers again. "Juanita, I want you to stay here in the library. I feel like having some champagne. Rutgar, would you care for a cocktail? Some Schnapps, perhaps?"

Rutgar smiled and said, "Chilled, if you have it."

"Naturally."

Svetlana entered the library wearing a belted wrap-around evening dress of emerald green. The dress was Katrina's, and being a wrap-around, the garment accommodated Svetlana's shorter but more curvaceous physique. All eyes turned toward her when she entered. Svetlana looked only at Katrina. She looked straight into the Russian's eyes, and didn't so much as blink as she crossed the room directly toward her.

"Thank you for inviting me to your lovely home," Svetlana said, her voice a sensual purr. She could tell that her directness had caught Katrina by surprise. "That dingy motel room was dreadful."

"You should have stayed here. There was no reason for you to leave."

Svetlana leaned forward and brushed her cheek against Katrina's, making a kissing sound as women so often did in public. The gesture, though far from intimate, also caught Katrina by surprise.

"Well, I'm here now," Svetlana replied. Then, in a much softer voice, she added, "That's all that matters, right?"

Also in a low tone that Rutgar could not hear, Katrina answered, "Yes, but touching my cheek with yours and kissing the air means you still haven't given me one good, real kiss."

From across the room, Rutgar pushed himself out of the easy chair he had been reclining in. "What's this whispering about? You'll make me think I'm missing out on something special."

Svetlana saw the anger flash in Katrina's icy eyes. The emotion was visible for a split second and no longer, but it had definitely been there, and Svetlana saw it for what it was. She turned toward the stranger and judged him immediately as a military man, a man of action. There was something about the way he held his body, the way he held his head and shoulders, that told her this was a hard, cruel man who knew what war and combat were all about—knew it intimately, and more importantly, enjoyed it.

"Svetlana, allow me to introduce you," Katrina said, taking Svetlana by the arm. "Rutgar, this is Svetlana. Svetlana, this is a professional acquaintance—Rutgar. He and his men will be staying here for a while to help me with business matters."

Rutgar's eyes did a slow perusal over Svetlana, which she pretended to not notice. Instead, she let her own cool gaze do the once-over of Katrina, who was stunning in the dark blue man-cut pantsuit.

"That's a beautiful look on you," Svetlana said to Katrina. "It shows your . . . power. Your personal discipline. It wouldn't work for me, but it works wonderfully for you."

Katrina's eyes began to smolder as she replied, "You're too generous with your compliments." She arched a brow and added, "If only you were so generous with everything you could give away . . . wouldn't that be lovely?"

Svetlana turned and saw Juanita standing near a small serving cart. "Juanita, is there any chilled champagne?" She crossed the room, moving away from Katrina. She felt the tall Russian's eyes upon her as she walked. She accepted a glass of champagne from Juanita, then said quietly, "Rutgar looks like a capable sort of fellow, doesn't he?"

"Everyone working for Comrade Luvesky is capable."

"That includes you?"

Juanita nodded. "Especially me. You're lucky you were able to sober up so quickly. If not, I'd have thrown you into a cold shower and let you shiver until you were sober. Make the cocktail you're drinking last a while. It's the only one I'll pour for you."

Twenty minutes later, after Svetlana had yawned several times, Katrina said, "Svetlana, why don't you go off to bed? Rutgar and I have much to discuss, and you don't need to bore yourself with business matters."

"I might find them interesting," Svetlana said brazenly, getting up out of the overstuffed chair she had been sitting in. She began crossing the room toward Katrina and Rutgar. "You never know."

"We're talking business. That's confidential. Now go to bed. You look exhausted. You need a good night's sleep." Katrina looked at her wristwatch. "It's almost four-thirty. Go on now. And don't be afraid to sleep late."

Svetlana looked at Katrina, then over to Rutgar. Yes, the two were definitely talking business . . . and they weren't going to let her in on the details.

"You're sure you don't mind me abandoning you?" Svetlana asked, as though requesting permission to leave.

"It's fine."

"Then a kiss, and I'm off to bed."

Svetlana was holding her champagne glass in her left hand as she moved a step closer to Katrina. She eased her right hand inside Katrina's unbuttoned jacket, sliding her palm over the Russian's ribs until she felt her spine through the thin barrier of the starched cotton shirt. With her high heels on, Katrina was many inches taller than the barefooted Svetlana.

"Good night," Svetlana whispered, leaning forward, pressing the heavy mounds of her D-cup breasts against Katrina as she tilted her face upward to receive a kiss.

Svetlana could tell that Katrina was shocked because of Svetlana's previous refusal to embark upon such intimacies. Katrina hesitated only a moment before slanting her mouth down over Svetlana's. When Svetlana's lips parted to invite a more intimate kiss, Katrina eased her tongue between them. Svetlana danced her tongue against the Russian's, sucking lightly, erotically on the woman's tongue.

Thirty seconds passed before Svetlana eased backward, ending the kiss. By the time she did, her cheeks were pink with a combination of embarrassment, passion, and an unacknowledged pleasure in exhibitionism. Katrina was also flushed, though the color in her cheeks was unquestionably because the flames of lust were heating her blood.

"Good night now," Svetlana said in a whisper, keeping her focus on Katrina while completely ignoring both Rutgar and Juanita. "I'll see you in the morning."

As Svetlana left the library, she felt certain that she had set a hook into Katrina. Now all she had to do was be patient and play it smart, and if she did, she would soon know who was really behind the murder of Sir Malcomb Sitwell, and what wild scheme Katrina Luvesky was putting in place in the Florida Keys.

In the morning, Svetlana awoke as the clock in the corner of the bedroom chimed softly. She blinked her eyes several times and was surprised to discover that it was already noon.

Svetlana could hear Rutgar's men working outside. They were laboring frantically to repair the damage Svetlana's firefight had caused to the mansion and the surrounding grounds. Standing at the window, wearing her panties and an oversized man's T-shirt, she watched as the mercenaries — and there was no doubt in her mind that these men were anything other than soldiers-for-hire — worked to plaster over bullet holes and repaint fresh patches in the sides of buildings.

Svetlana watched the hired killers working to patch the rear wall of one boathouse. *We all used silencers. Only the flash-bang grenade caused any real noise. Before the sun goes down tonight, there won't be a single bit of visual evidence to show that last night there was a furious gun battle involving fully automatic weapons.*

Svetlana pushed herself away from the window. She was once again inside the compound, surrounded by people who would kill her if they ever learned she was a sanctioned killer for a mysterious department of the United States known as Omega Force. It was an eerie thing, to be distinctly aware that every person surrounding her would murder her on a moment's notice should they ever discover who and what she really was.

But what Svetlana also knew, even though she struggled desperately to deny this awareness from her consciousness, that it was playing the game of deception — it was getting inside the belly of the beast that she was trying to kill — that gave her life meaning and purpose and excitement. The thrill she felt in being a field agent on assignment for Omega Force was so strong, so all-consuming, it was almost sexual in nature.

What to wear, Svetlana mused, thinking about Katrina.

All she was certain of was that she had to pick something that was casual and modest enough to allow her to walk around in, yet flirtatious and tempting enough to keep the hook of sexual frustration, which she had implanted into Katrina Luvesky the previous night, securely in place.

Katrina was annoyed that she'd overlooked something. It was always a bad sign to overlook anything, of course, but to over-look something as fundamental as language . . .well, that was really inexcusable. And the blame rested completely upon her own shoulders.

"But you can speak English, right?" she asked one of Rut-gar's men.

The man nodded, but looking into his eyes, Katrina could tell that he didn't know enough English to understand that she wanted him to put the plaster on the mansion's siding thicker so that it would completely cover up any sign of the building being sprayed with machine gun fire.

"Damn it," Katrina muttered to herself as she turned away from the broad-shouldered young man.

Movement from her left drew Katrina's attention. When she looked in that direction, her breath caught in her throat. Svetlana was standing alone in the middle of the lawn, bathed in sunlight, looking for someone. Katrina silently hoped that she was the someone Svetlana was searching for.

Though Svetlana was gorgeous every time that Katrina had seen her, never before had the American looked quite so appealing, quite so delectable. Svetlana wore a tight-fitting red tank top with spaghetti shoulder straps. The clingy

garment hugged her curves and defined the shape and fullness of her breasts which—it was lusciously obvious—were
unencumbered by a brassiere. Beneath the form-fitting tank
top, Svetlana had opted for well-washed denim cut-off shorts
that showed off her legs to their best advantage. Her luxurious blonde hair glowed healthily in the brilliant Florida sunlight, flowing over her shoulders and down her back, the
silken strands moving with the breeze.

Svetlana turned her face slowly toward Katrina. When she
saw the tall Russian, she broke into a beaming smile. Though
Svetlana did not run to close the distance that separated her
from Katrina, her stride was much more hurried than a mere
leisurely walk. Because she had deliberately chosen to leave
her bedroom without wearing a brassiere, Svetlana's heavy
breasts moved with freedom inside the lightweight tank top.
Her nipples were hard little buds of flesh that drew Katrina's
heated gaze like an erotic magnet.

"I can't believe I slept so late," Svetlana exclaimed as she
approached. "How long have you been up and working?"

"Not really all that long," Katrina answer. She had lied.
Katrina had been too anxious to get the new men fixing the
American headquarters of the Moscow Cartel for her to re-
main alone in bed any longer than was absolutely necessary.

It took every ounce of willpower she possessed to keep
from reaching out and squeezing the twin mounds of Svetlana's breasts. Katrina almost salivated at the thought of tast-
ing those nipples without having the infuriating barrier of
clothing separating her tongue from Svetlana's responsive
skin. Vividly detailed memories of the thrills she'd had earlier
experienced surged through Katrina's brain. She remembered
how Svetlana shivered, and how her nipples became hard as
she sucked them through the lingerie's sheer silk bodice.

"I've got to talk to you," Svetlana explained, her voice dipping low. She glanced to her left. A solidly built German was

striding quickly across the vast green lawn, headed straight for Katrina. "Privately."

"Of course. I'm very busy now but perhaps just a little later we could . . ."

Svetlana's eyes appeared filled with confusion and anxiety. She moistened her lips with the tip of her tongue and whispered hurriedly, "It's about last night. I . . . I don't know what came over me. You see I don't . . . I mean I'm not . . ."

The German mercenary stepped close enough and gave his head a slight nod. He behaved with Katrina as a soldier would when addressing a superior officer. "We need your opinion regarding work on the boathouse."

"The back of the boathouse?"

"Yes, Comrade Luvesky."

"I'll be there in just a moment." Katrina waited until the muscular soldier, new to the headquarters of the Moscow Cartel, walked away. Then she turned her attention back to Svetlana, saying, "There was nothing wrong with what happened between us last night. You must know that."

Svetlana's gaze darted left and right, as though she was speaking of things that were horrifically embarrassing to her. "Only once before have I . . . you know what I'm talking about."

"I'm not sure that I do," Katrina replied, enjoying her guest's unease. "Why don't you tell me? Be specific so that there are no unfortunate misunderstandings. I'm Russian, after all, and English is my second language."

"Last night . . . well, you just don't understand about last night."

Katrina was smiling contentedly as she nodded her head slowly. "Very well. I'm too busy right now, but I should be able to free up a little time later on."

Svetlana sighed, and her breasts wobbled tautly inside the tank top. Her breasts drew Katrina's gaze. Katrina made no effort to hide either the direction of her gaze, or the heated emotion going through her.

Rutgar was crossing the lawn toward Katrina as Svetlana started to turn and walked away, but Katrina saw the slightest hint of a smile on her lips.

Katrina was inspecting the patching job that Rutgar's men had done on the siding of the automobile garage. Even though she was quite willing to proclaim Rutgar and his men incompetent of the task if necessary, she had to admit to herself—and even more importantly, to Rutgar—that the repair job had been handled with a level of craftsmanship that was nearly professional in its skill. Not bad at all, considering the men who had repaired the bullet holes in the building's siding had much more experience creating havoc with bullets than hiding the effect of those bullets.

"I'm impressed," Katrina said at last, turning toward Rutgar. "Your men have proven themselves to be loyal and versatile. That makes them valuable to the Moscow Cartel. We make men wealthy when they're valuable."

She looked into Rutgar's eyes, wondering if he, a German who spoke English as a second language, understood all the subtle implications of what she—a Russian who spoke English as a second language—was saying. For several seconds she looked into his eyes. It was when looking into his eyes that Katrina read the underlying disdain the German assassin felt whenever taking orders, or even compliments, from a woman. Especially one with a Russian accent.

She smiled and added, "Mr. Bigg will hear of your skill and professionalism. Mr. Bigg never forgets the men who go the extra kilometer. He knows what it takes to see that an operation runs smoothly."

It wasn't until Katrina had mentioned Mr. Bigg's name that she saw any real enthusiasm in Rutgar's eyes. It was at that precise moment that she realized Rutgar would never have any real respect for her as a leader, no matter what she accomplished. But as long as Rutgar thought he was following Mr. Bigg's orders — not Katrina's — he would remain a faithful and effective soldier for the Moscow Cartel.

"Do you want us to repair the inside as well?" Rutgar asked.

"No, I don't care what the inside of the garage looks like. So long as the bullet holes are hidden from the outside, that's all that matters."

Katrina was about to say more but was stopped when she heard a woman's high-pitched squeal of pain. Standing at the doorway to the four-car garage, Katrina turned to see Vlad half-pulling and half-dragging Svetlana toward the garage. His massive right hand was wrapped around her left biceps as he pulled her along. Svetlana was struggling, occasionally losing her balance in her high heels. Twice she hit Vlad's forearm, but the blows were completely ineffectual. Walking behind Vlad and Svetlana was Juanita, whose expression was grim, tinged with contempt.

"What is this?" Katrina asked. She kept her gaze away from Svetlana as a thousand suspicions regarding the tempting vixen exploded in her brain.

"Vlad caught her sneaking around the boathouse," Juanita explained, stepping forward past Svetlana and the mute Russian giant.

"Which boathouse?"

"The new one."

Katrina's eyes narrowed. The new boathouse concealed the mini submarine. She looked at Svetlana, avoiding the woman's gaze. Had the lust she felt for Svetlana weakened her judgment? It was a question Katrina hated asking of herself, but one which she felt she could not now avoid.

Svetlana began to speak. Katrina snapped her fingers. An

instant later, Vlad clamped an enormous hand over Svetlana's mouth. He held her tightly against his body with his left arm, his right hand keeping her protests silent.

"Did she see inside the boathouse?"

"No, Comrade Luvesky."

"You're sure."

"Yes."

"Release her. Leave. All of you, leave now."

"But she could be dangerous, Comrade Luvesky."

Katrina's lips curled disdainfully as she looked at Svetlana. "I will interrogate her. If she doesn't have the proper answers, I'll have Vlad squeeze the answers out of her."

Juanita smiled.

When Katrina was alone in the garage with Svetlana, she stepped close, forcing the much shorter woman to look up to see into her face.

"You'd better have the right answers to my questions," Katrina said softly, her voice like the hiss of a poisonous snake. "If you don't, I'll have Vlad put his hands to your ears and then watch as he crushes your skull. Have you ever watched a person die in such a fashion?"

"No. Of course not," Svetlana replied. She took a step backward and was stopped by the front left fender of a Chevrolet Suburban. She could retreat no farther.

Katrina closed the distance again, standing less than twelve inches from her guest. She looked into Svetlana's emerald green eyes, then down into the woman's tempting cleavage. The sight of the twin pale mounds of feminine flesh was alluring to Katrina. She lusted after Svetlana, but simultaneously she was fearful that her hunger for the American was clouding her judgment and weakening her discipline.

"Why were you snooping around the new boathouse?" Katrina asked. She was studying Svetlana's expression, searching for any sign of duplicity.

"We need to talk," Svetlana said softly. "There are men everywhere. I was looking for some place where we could talk in private."

"You have your own room in the mansion," Katrina replied sharply. "What's wrong with that?"

"That's a bedroom," Svetlana said softly, emphasizing the key word. "When we were together in the hallway, I think I may have misled you. I'm not trying to pretend that I'm some silly little virgin. I've been with men before."

"What about with women?"

"Y-Yes," Svetlana stammered. "But just once. And I was very, very drunk at the time. I guess I drink too much whenever I'm depressed or confused, and that's how it happened." Svetlana's expression said she ached for sympathy. "I didn't kiss you. Not really kiss, anyway. You said so yourself. That's what made you so angry — remember?"

"It's true that I didn't kiss your mouth." Katrina brushed Svetlana's nipples through the thin tank top with the backs of her knuckles. Svetlana gasped once again, drawing yet another chuckle from Katrina. "I did kiss your nipples, though. They got hard for me. It felt good, and you know it. You also know that it'll feel even better if I suck on your bare nipples instead of trying to chew my way through silk lingerie."

Svetlana pushed Katrina's hand away from her breast. "Stop," she said weakly. "I'm serious. I'm stone cold sober and I only like men."

"My kisses make you drunk," Katrina bragged. "My kisses make you wet. That's why you squirm about like a teenage virgin."

"Stop it, damn you!"

Katrina placed her hand over Svetlana's left breast at exactly the same moment that she kissed Svetlana hard on the mouth to silence any further protests. She caught Svetlana's nipple through the thin barrier of the tank top and pinched with cruel strength. As she forced her tongue between Svetlana's lips to begin the French kissing that she had hungered for, Katrina released Svetlana's nipple. She thrust her hand up beneath the tank top to at last feel the plump, luscious breast in all its naked glory.

All suspicion Katrina had that the American was harboring secrets vanished. When Katrina pressed her fingers deeply into the Svetlana's breast and danced her tongue slowly and sensually against the woman's tongue, her better judgment evaporated. French kissing Svetlana — and believing that she was the first woman ever to kiss her passionately without the inhibition-dulling effects of liquor — was such a turn-on for Katrina that she could feel her panties clinging to the lips of her own rapidly moistening femininity. It wasn't until Svetlana forcibly turned her face aside that the first soulful French kiss finally ended.

"Stop! Wait! You don't understand!" Svetlana gasped.

But Katrina did understand. She understood that Svetlana did not want to become passionately excited because of another woman's kiss. She understood that Svetlana believed experiencing lesbian passion was somehow wrong. She understood that Svetlana's passion was burning out of control, just as Katrina's own passion was burning . . .and it was being conscious of all this, knowing that she was turning on a woman who did not want to be aroused, that sent Katrina into a fever-pitch of excitement.

"I understand everything, you spoiled American bitch!" Katrina said sharply. She shoved her hand up between Svetlana's thighs, rubbing firmly through the impediment of cotton bikini panties and denim short shorts. "I'm tired of understanding. It's time for you to obey orders, and suffer if you don't!"

Katrina was frantic to get inside Svetlana's cut-off jeans. She nearly ripped the garment in her haste to unfasten the brass snap and pull down the barely inch-long zipper. An instant later she thrust her hand inside the tight-fitting garment. Her hand slid inside the waistband of Svetlana's panties, her fingertips brushing over the velvety-soft hair . . .and then — at last — she was touching the pink sex lips that had caused Katrina to toss and turn with restless dreams.

"American bitch!" the Russian hissed. She bared her teeth and bit Svetlana's neck with enough savagery to create a bruise and elicit a sharp cry of pain. "I'll teach you to play games with Katrina Luvesky!"

Katrina felt the warm, slick honey of Svetlana's passion against her fingertips. It was all the evidence she needed to realize that though the American's words were in protest to the dominating seduction, her body was in complete acceptance. Abject and total surrender to eroticism was no longer in question. Katrina knew satisfaction was just a matter of time. Boldly, arrogantly, almost cruelly, she thrust her middle finger upward between the lips of Svetlana's tender pink cunt.

Svetlana cried out in surprise and desire. She squeezed her eyes shut and grabbed Katrina's wrist, though she did not make the effort to push the hand out of her short shorts. The finger slipped between passion-enflamed lips.

"Get down!" Katrina hissed, grabbing Svetlana by the shoulders. "Get down, arrogant American bitch!"

Katrina pushed down hard on Svetlana's shoulders, forcing her to sit on the running board of the Suburban. When Katrina looked down, it was wildly thrilling to see Svetlana's pale, upturned face, her bountiful cleavage inside the tight-fitting tank top, and the wild array of disheveled golden hair that was silky soft and carried the fragrance of fine shampoo.

"You're going to kiss me. Kiss me until I tell you to stop!" Katrina whispered feverishly as she worked frantically to unbuckle her own belt. "Lick, damn you."

It was Rutgar's voice that destroyed the moment and ended the encounter with Svetlana. The German stuck his head inside the garage and called out, "Comrade Luvesky, we need your advice regarding the underwater hoist support."

Katrina uttered a Russian obscenity under her breath. She was mostly hidden from Rutgar's view by the Suburban. Svetlana was completely hidden, a fact for which Katrina was thankful.

"I'll be right there," Katrina said after a moment.

Rutgar asked, "Is there anything I can help you with?"

"No, Rutgar. Go back to what you were doing. I'll be there in just a moment."

"Yes, Comrade Luvesky."

Katrina was breathing deeply, her breasts rising and falling. Slowly, while looking down at Svetlana, who remained seated on the Suburban's running board, Katrina refastened her belt properly.

"Work," Katrina whispered, her breathing slowly returning to normal. "It's always work. But soon it won't be. Soon I'll give orders to those goose-stepping Germans that we are not to be disturbed no matter what." Katrina reached down and wound a lock of Svetlana's long, silky hair around a fingertip. "Very soon I'm going to need someone to drive a car for me. Someone I can trust. Will you be that person for me?" Katrina's cool gaze was intense, boring into the seated woman. "Don't disappoint me, Svetlana. You've done that too many times already."

Long seconds ticked silently by. The Russian looked unwaveringly into Svetlana's eyes.

Svetlana at last answered, "I'll drive the car, if that's what you want me to do. I'll do anything you say."

Katrina smiled. "Smart girl."

Arturo was ashen faced, his gaze darting from Katrina to Vlad to Juanita to Rutgar . . .then always back to the undisputed leader of the gigantic, unsmiling Russian.

"Very curious that you were shot with some kind of dart that rendered you unconscious, but everyone else — every single one of your comrades in arms — was shot to death. I find that very curious." Katrina looked Arturo up and down briefly, then turned away from him and studied the mini submarine. "If Rutgar hadn't been able to get here so quickly with his men, the Moscow Cartel's American headquarters would have been terribly understaffed, wouldn't it?"

Arturo didn't answer. Vlad, standing behind him, nudged Arturo, who then said, "Yes, Comrade Luvesky! Of course!"

"You have failed me, Arturo." Katrina turned once more to face the petrified underling. "You have failed Mr. Bigg. You have failed the Moscow Cartel. You have failed your fellow soldiers in arms." Katrina raised her right hand slowly to shoulder height, her gaze locked with Arturo's. She snapped her fingers. Vlad immediately put his palms over Arturo's ears, trapping his head between his hands. "Svetlana will take your place for me. You are no longer necessary."

Arturo began to struggle, but it was futile. Vlad lifted him by his head and began squeezing. Arturo's face contorted as the excruciating pain jolted his senses. A moment later his skull shattered. Blood sluiced from his eye sockets and nostrils. With a single, savage twist and shake, Vlad superfluously broke the man's neck. He held Arturo's corpse as though it was weightless, though the toes dangled several inches above the floor.

Katrina looked at Rutgar, who was white-faced. He had never before witnessed Katrina's favorite method of discipline.

"That's what happens to soldiers who have failed Mr. Bigg." Katrina smiled. She had made her point, and Rutgar would explain to his men what had happened to Arturo. Every one of the Germans would be particularly willing to serve Katrina in any capacity necessary, never asking questions, never doubting her authority. "Vlad, get rid of the body. Juanita, we transfer the next shipment tomorrow night. I want to go over contingency plans once again."

"In the library, Comrade Luvesky?"

"Yes, but after we eat. I seem to have worked up quite an appetite." She smiled.

CHAPTER ELEVEN

B urke sat in his hotel room, staring out the window. Though he was sitting in the heart of Washington D.C., his thoughts were of a faraway place that he'd never been to — the Florida Keys.

What had happened to Svetlana Simonov? That question had been on his thoughts constantly.

His telephone buzzed, and he closed his eyes for a moment. He didn't feel like talking to anyone, and he thought for several seconds of simply pretending that the telephone hadn't buzzed at all. It buzzed a second, then third time, and finally he lifted the telephone off the cradle.

"This is Burke!" he said sharply, not at all pleased that he had been disturbed.

"Sir, Osborne here. You asked to be informed immediately if we received any contact on Security Line Six. We have, sir."

Burke felt his heart skip a beat. He asked, "What did she report?"

"She requested GR-3. One full pound's worth. I can get the drop-off point if you'd like, sir."

GR-3 was a special incendiary chemical developed by Omega Force. The chemical — a fine powder, actually — burned at an extraordinarily high temperature. So hot, in fact, that it tended to completely burn away all evidence of the incendiary device that had created the fire. Furthermore, with an extremely small charge placed inside the package, the powder spread in a deadly halo before igniting. With a remote control, an absolute inferno could be started from several hundred yards away.

Burke asked, "She received what she requested?"

"As an in-field agent? Of course, sir. She got it immediately. Our man found the perfect nearby drop point for her. Standard operating procedure, sir."

"Yes, yes, of course."

"It's going to get hot in south Florida, sir."

Burke smiled and replied, "Yes, I'm sure it's going to get hot as hell very soon."

He broke off the connection, kicked his feet up onto his desk, and let himself smile broadly. Why would Svetlana Simonov request a high-tech incendiary powder? Though Burke didn't have a single piece of solid evidence to back up his opinion, he had a feeling that very soon the persons responsible for Sir Malcomb Sitwell's murder would be paying for their crime. They might have eluded the law enforcement agencies of Florida and the United States, but they hadn't eluded Svetlana Simonov . . .and her brand of justice was much swifter and more final than any a court and judge in the United States would invoke.

Svetlana Simonov was leaning back in an overstuffed chair in the library. More than twenty-four hours earlier, Katrina had tried desperately to seduce Svetlana in the mansion's multicar garage. Since that time, Svetlana had learned that her job duties for a mysterious organization called the Moscow Cartel would be to drive a sedan to a specific location, get out of the car, walk to another car, and drive that car back to headquarters.

Though Svetlana still did not have a complete understanding of all that Katrina Luvesky had going, she now knew much more than she had just a day earlier. Svetlana had learned that Katrina was not the boss of the entire operation.

There was someone named Mr. Bigg who actually pulled all the strings and ran the whole show. Katrina answered to Mr. Bigg, but to no one else. The mere mention of Mr. Bigg's name caused strong men—even seasoned soldiers, like Rutgar—to quiver in their boots.

Though Svetlana had not been told that there would be drugs in the trunk of the car that she would be driving, it didn't take long to come to the inevitable conclusion that Katrina Luvesky was a drug trafficker. Not the basic, run-of-the-mill drug trafficker, to be sure, but a drug dealer nevertheless. Svetlana was almost disheartened that Katrina was nothing more than a criminal—albeit an uncommon criminal. Organized and efficient, to be sure, running the Moscow Cartel like a Fortune 500 company . . .but still, all in all, just another greedy criminal who lived by killing, stealing, and lying her way through this world.

The library door opened, drawing Svetlana's attention. Vlad's enormous body filled the doorway. The sight of him caused the breath to catch in her throat, just as it always did whenever she looked at him. Never had she seen anyone who was so large, nor had she seen anyone who so appeared to be the personification of a mythical evil giant. When she looked into his eyes—and that was something that she tried to avoid whenever possible—she saw nothing that was human. Nothing at all. He was the type of man—more like a monster, really—who could kill without thinking about it. It seemed to Svetlana that killing for Vlad wasn't something that he either enjoyed or disliked. Instead, it was something that he could do because of the sheer size of his physical presence, but he had no emotion about it one way or the other.

To Svetlana, he seemed to be lacking in almost all of the known human emotions. He was not savage. Not sadistic. He was just heartless. Not so much human as machine-like.

"What is it, Vlad?"

He raised a hand and motioned for her to follow him.

"Where are we going?"

Again, he made the same motion.

"I want to know where we're going," Svetlana said with more vehemence.

The look that Vlad gave Svetlana warned her that either she would come along peaceably, or he would take her with him by force.

"All right," Svetlana replied, closing a paperback book and putting it aside. "If you insist. But I'm letting you know right now, Katrina—Comrade Luvesky, I mean—is going to hear about this."

For the first time in her life, Svetlana saw Vlad smile. It wasn't a smile, actually. Just a twitch on the left corner of his mouth. But it had been caused by an emotion, and the notion that an emotion had gone through Vlad was enough to make Svetlana begin to worry.

Katrina inhaled the line of cocaine deeply into her left nostril. The cocaine had been chopped up into a fine powder and put into lines on the mirror. There had been eight lines on the mirror earlier. There were only four lines left.

She turned toward the bed. When she turned, the whole world seemed to spin a little, wiggling and swirling momentarily before becoming stable again. Katrina smiled. The marijuana was first-rate, and so was the cocaine. Marijuana to calm the ambitions, relax the spirit, free up the inhibitions, and cocaine to fire up the senses to all the glorious possibilities of pleasure. Then, to top it all off, a couple pills of Ecstasy washed down with icy cold 1983 Dom Perignon champagne, and Katrina Luvesky was set for the evening.

Juanita was on the bed, resting on her side. More precisely, she was on the beds. Two king sized mattresses had been put together, and Katrina had hired a seamstress to sew custom-made fitted silk sheets for the enormous surface. It wasn't a bed so much as a wrestling mat, Katrina decided, and the mental image this prompted caused her to giggle like a misbehaving little girl.

Juanita's slender, naked body looked delicious in the dim light. And she did, in fact, taste delicious. Katrina knew this with certainty, since she had been nibbling on Juanita, in one fashion or another, for the past half hour.

Katrina looked at the young woman. *Stoned! I'm so completely stoned!* It was a comfort to know that Juanita would do anything to please her. Knowing she had complete power over another human being made Katrina amorous. *But I'm not going to worry about being stoned. Not tonight. I've got every one of Rutgar's men on duty, and they're top quality men armed to defend this property against anything. Tonight, all I've got to worry about is me. I'm all that matters. Nothing else in the whole world matters but me, and that's just the way it should be.*

Juanita was not smiling. She almost never smiled, Katrina realized. Sometimes, when Katrina was alone with Juanita, she thought it might be nice if they could just talk as friends would. Instead they maintained the master-slave relationship that existed between them.

You're stoned! You don't need friends! You need workers, and that's what you've got! It's Juanita's job to make you happy. That's what you pay her to do. It's as simple as that. You own the girl's body and soul, and you can do with her whatever you like.

Katrina got onto the bed. Juanita moved so that Katrina could sit in the very middle of the bed, with her back against the mound of pillows pushed up against the headboard. Katrina was completely naked, her nipples still moist from Juanita's wet, tender kisses that had been administered with precision minutes earlier.

"You've found very good medicine," Katrina said to Juanita. Katrina never used the word *drugs* in conjunction to her own consumption. She reached out and pushed her fingers into Juanita's long, black, silky hair, caressing the strands. "You're my most—"

Katrina was silenced when the bedroom door opened wide. The hallway was dark. The bedroom was illuminated only by a dozen squat, delicately scented candles. The shadowed image that filled the doorway could be none other than Vlad—Vlad the Impaler had returned, and he had brought Svetlana Simonov with him!

"Come in, Vlad," Katrina commanded quietly.

The giant stepped into the room. When Svetlana walked in, he closed the door behind her. Katrina could tell that Svetlana's eyes had not yet become accustomed to the dim light. Katrina smiled. Soon enough Svetlana would be able to see quite clearly, and when that happened, Katrina would know whether the American woman with the extraordinary bosom and face of an angel would follow orders and provide pleasure, or would not follow orders and would therefore have to be punished. Either way, Katrina's satisfaction was guaranteed. Sometimes it was even more of a turn-on to administer pain than be the recipient of pleasure.

Svetlana wore a cotton dress of robin's egg blue. The hem came down to the middle of her shapely thighs, and the décolletage was a bit on the daring side. Katrina had sent Svetlana shopping that morning, handing her a fistful of bills, stating that she wanted Svetlana to pick up clothes that made her easy on the eyes. Svetlana stood at the foot of the bed, blinking her eyes. Katrina watched as she at first became aware of the hazy outline of bodies on the bed before her, then saw in greater detail her surroundings.

"Good evening, Svetlana," Katrina purred silkily. "I'm glad that you've come to join us."

Svetlana's jaw dropped open when she saw that Katrina and Juanita were in bed together, and that both were naked.

Vlad had moved over toward the door. Svetlana glanced at Vlad as though suspecting it was his job to prevent her from making an escape. Vlad, though, was unbuttoning his shirt and slipping if off while he stepped out of his enormous shoes.

"But, Katrina, I didn't think that—"

"That's right, darling," Katrina said quickly, cutting the woman's statement off. "There's no reason for you to think. I'll do that for you." She turned her attention toward Juanita and said, "Give Svetlana a helping hand, will you?"

Juanita slipped soundlessly off the bed. She weighed a mere hundred pounds, and when she put her feet to the floor and took her weight off the bed, the mattress hardly moved at all. Her breasts were firm, small mounds, capped by dark brown areolas the size of silver dollars. Her nipples were blunt-tipped and erect. Naked, she appeared even younger and more petite than she did with clothes on. Juanita walked to Svetlana. She was naturally inches shorter than Svetlana, and with the American wearing high heels, she appeared even more diminutive.

"Turn toward me," Katrina purred. "I want to look at both of you a moment, side by side."

Juanita turned toward the bed, and Katrina's heart skipped a beat. Svetlana and Juanita were startling contrasts to each other. Juanita stood there unashamed and completely naked, her luscious, tanned body all sleek, smooth lines without an ounce extra of weight, while Svetlana wore the attractive blue dress that Katrina had paid for, her bountiful bosom swelling out in a low-cut décolletage, her luxurious hair shimmering healthily, her curves dramatic and strikingly feminine, even when hidden with clothes. And Svetlana was nervous. Katrina could tell . . .and it excited her.

"That's one of the new outfits I asked you to buy?"

Svetlana nodded. She looked at Katrina, then at Juanita.

When she looked at Vlad, who was standing naked near the door, she turned her face away so quickly her long hair swirled around her cheeks and shoulders.

Katrina looked over at Vlad to see what had shocked Svetlana so. Vlad was standing completely naked at the door. He was always impressive to look at—seven feet tall and over three hundred pounds. But seeing him naked, with his massive chest and tree trunk-like legs and arms, he was truly spectacular. Especially when one saw his cock. Even though his phallus was slumbering, it hung between his thighs, long and thick. To a feminine psyche, it was more than just a little disconcerting.

"He can be intimidating to look at," Katrina said with a smile. "I remember the first time I saw him naked. I thought I'd die. But I didn't die. I simply had more orgasms that night than I thought I was capable of." She looked at Svetlana through mascara-darkened eyelashes, her eyes barely open. "If you're a very good girl, I might even let you have some of Vlad. He really is something special."

"That won't be necessary," Svetlana said, finding her voice after several seconds.

"That's not for you to decide." She kept a distinct undercurrent in her tone that warned everyone in the room that her orders would be followed precisely, or punishment of a profoundly painful nature would be dispensed. "I'll decide who gives pleasure and who receives pleasure. Is that clear?"

Svetlana did not respond.

Katrina icily added, "That is clear to you, isn't it, Svetlana? You understand that from now on I'll be making all your decisions for you."

"Y-Yes," Svetlana replied, appearing completely disoriented by the situation. "Of course. Naturally."

"That's more like it. Now take your clothes off." Katrina snapped her fingers. "Juanita, give Svetlana a helping hand.

And don't be in too much of a hurry. We have all the time in the world."

"Yes, Comrade Luvesky."

Juanita turned toward Svetlana once again, and without saying a word, reached for the buttons at the curvaceous woman's bodice. Svetlana's hands came up quickly, as though by their own volition without any conscious thought on her part. She grabbed Juanita's slender wrists.

"Don't be a fool." Katrina snapped. Her tone softened as she added, "We're all here to have fun, so do be accommodating, Svetlana. Juanita is only trying to help, and I can tell you from experience that she may be frightfully young and tiny as a pixie, but she's exquisitely skilled." Katrina's right hand was between her own thighs. She was touching herself absent-mindedly. "You've behaved badly toward Juanita. I think you should kiss her to show her you're sorry."

Katrina was jealous of all her lovers, but there was also a warring streak of voyeurism in her. It was her voyeurism that turned her on to watch other people having sex. It was her thirst for power over other people that made her so hot and wet whenever she could demand that someone — like Svetlana, for instance — do something that they clearly did not want to do.

In a deeper, more authoritative tone, Katrina said, "Don't make me have to ask you again, Svetlana. Kiss Juanita. Let me see how you kiss her. I want to be able to see from that kiss that you're truly sorry for the way you have just behaved."

Svetlana released Juanita's wrists. She smiled slightly, her gaze dancing from Katrina to Juanita.

"I'm sorry," Svetlana said, loudly enough that Katrina could hear. "I was surprised, that's all. Not offended. Just surprised."

She bent down to kiss Juanita. When she did, the naked girl wound her slender arms around Svetlana's neck. They kissed with closed mouths, neither one attempting to make the first kiss a deeply probing one.

Juanita ended the kiss, and hugged Svetlana more tightly. She put her lips close to Svetlana's ear, her mouth hidden from Katrina's view.

"Listen carefully," Juanita said, whispering. Her tone was cold as ice, deadly as arsenic. "This night isn't about your satisfaction. You mean nothing. You are here for the same reason that I am — because Comrade Katrina Luvesky wants you here to give her pleasure. What you want or do not want does not matter. All that matters is Comrade Luvesky, and her enjoyment. Displease her, and you'll answer to me . . .you capitalist bitch!"

Katrina demanded, "No whispering! Juanita, you know I don't like it when you keep secrets from me."

Juanita said under her breath to Svetlana, "Make Comrade Luvesky unhappy and I'll cut you to pieces and feed you to the sharks." Then she turned toward Katrina and added aloud, "What do you want me to do now? You know we'll do anything you want."

"You're sure she doesn't mind you touching her?"

"I think not." Juanita put her hand over Svetlana's breast, squeezing the plump mound through the dress and brassiere. "She's very big. And firm. I think you'll like touching her, Comrade Luvesky."

"Take her clothes off for me, Juanita," Katrina purred. The tips of her right fingers moved in a slow, circular motion between her legs as she rubbed the center of all her most sensitive nerve endings. Situations like this one made her clit particularly responsive. "This is the second time that I've had to ask you."

"Yes, Comrade Luvesky."

"And Svetlana, I don't want you to fight her, but don't help her, either. I want you to be . . .a present. A beautiful birthday present that I'm watching being unwrapped. Yes, that's what you are . . .a present I'm giving to myself. I've worked so very hard. I deserve to have you. I deserve this night."

As Juanita began slowly unbuttoning the front of Svetlana's dress, Katrina reached over for the ash tray, found the marijuana cigarette, and lit it with a butane lighter. She took one large inhalation from the cigarette, then set it aside. It wouldn't do to get too stoned. On two or three occasions, she had gotten too high to truly enjoy herself, and that not only made her feel as though she had cheated herself out of the orgasms because they would not happen, but also made her feel weak—and Katrina Luvesky, leader of the Moscow Cartel, despised weakness in everyone, most especially in herself.

Katrina watched, studying every subtle nuance of expression that flickered across Svetlana's lovely face. When the dress was completely unbuttoned, Juanita pushed it over Svetlana's shoulders and down to the fully rounded curve of her hips, then to her ankles. Katrina smiled broadly. Encircling Svetlana's waist was a black, lacy garter belt, which held up thigh-high black silk stockings. Her brassiere was black, and so were the sheer bikini panties that covered her most intimate area.

"I must say, I approve of the way you spend my money," Katrina purred, her eyes smoldering with lust. "Black looks so good against your fair skin. Very, very nice. I've always had an appreciation for very feminine women who know enough to wear lingerie that flatters their charms."

Juanita began to unfasten the clasp of Svetlana's brassiere, but Katrina stopped her with a motion of her hand. "Pull the cups beneath her breasts, if you can," Katrina said thoughtfully, like a fashion designer making a last-minute adjustment on her latest creation before the model walked out onto the runway. "I like the way the dark fabric looks against her skin."

Once again, Svetlana gasped in surprise. This time it was when Juanita who calmly but insistently pushed her hand inside the brassiere and tugged Svetlana's plump right breast upward as she pulled the sheer cup of the brassiere downward. She repeated the process with Svetlana's other breast, leaving the brassiere beneath the naked, exposed twin mounds.

"Your breasts are almost too large," Katrina said thoughtfully, her heart fluttering as she looked at Svetlana's naked bosom for the very first time. "Almost, but not quite. Most women wouldn't look good with breasts that large, but you seem to manage it. You're really quite lucky, you know."

Katrina glanced to her right. Vlad was standing passively, in the at-ease position with his feet spread to shoulder's width and his hands clasped together behind his back. His posture made it obvious that his enormous phallus was growing, stretching out, becoming greater in length and girth. His professionalism allowed him to stand at-ease and not openly gawk at the beautiful woman being disrobed in front of him, but his body and his lusts were not so dispassionate regarding such things.

"Vlad approves of how you look, too." Katrina laughed softly. It was a tittering laugh, almost like that of a little girl. But it was the laugh of a powerful woman in the throes of an assortment of very powerful mood-altering drugs. "I can see that from here. But then, a woman doesn't have to get very close to Vlad to know what he's thinking."

She laughed more forcefully then, her breasts jiggling on her chest, tears of laughter rolling down her cheeks. When she recovered, she turned her attention back toward the two women standing at the foot of her enormous bed, then over to the Russian giant.

"Vlad, come closer. There's no reason for you to stand at the door," Katrina said when she had recovered some of her composure. She looked at Svetlana's heavy breasts and sighed softly, contentedly, like a love-struck girl might upon seeing a movie star. "So beautiful . . .but look at her breasts! The nipples are not erect! Not like mine are, and not like Juanita's." In a gesture befitting an empress, Katrina snapped her fingers. "Juanita! Vlad! Make the woman's nipples stand at attention!"

The startled cry that came from Svetlana's throat, despite her obvious intentions of remaining silent, was music in Katrina's ears. Katrina watched as Svetlana squirmed in abject embarrassment while Juanita and Vlad began sucking on her nipples. Svetlana stood there, silent and unmoving, while the two loyal soldiers of the Moscow Cartel used their lips and tongues upon her responsive nipples. As the two soldiers nibbled upon Svetlana's tender breasts, her expression was a bizarre mixture of intense pleasure and overwhelming embarrassment. Katrina could not have been more pleased.

When Juanita and Vlad moved away from Svetlana to show Katrina their handiwork, Svetlana's nipples were fiercely erect in the center of her large areolas. Katrina smiled. Svetlana was getting turned on. That much was obvious from the blush on the woman's cheeks. Even in the pale candlelight, it was clear that Svetlana, though furious at being ordered about and treated badly, was getting aroused.

I wonder if she'd like a spanking? I know I'd like giving her a spanking . . .on the bare bottom . . .with someone watching us. It's always so much better whenever there's an audience.

Vlad eased his fingers inside the waistband of Svetlana's panties on the left side. Juanita put her tiny hand into the panties on the right side. Together, they looked to their leader for guidance. Katrina's mouth tightened into a cruel line. She nodded. Without hesitation, Vlad and Juanita pulled apart. Another high, startled cry of surprise was emitted from Svetlana, this time because her new bikini panties had been ripped from her body. She immediately covered her most private area with her hands.

"Don't be shy," Katrina snapped. She sat up a bit straighter in the bed, pushing herself backward against the pillows piled against the headboard. "And come to me, darling. It's time that you kiss me like you love me. Stop avoiding the inevitable."

For several seconds, Svetlana stood motionless at the foot of the bed. She was as erotic a vision as Katrina had ever seen, standing there with those spectacular breasts lifted up above the cups of her straining brassiere, her nipples and areolas wet from the mouths of Juanita and Vlad the Impaler, her slender waist tapering in dramatically before the hips flared outward. Between the pale white thighs there was the small, rectangular mound of pubic hair shimmering auburn-brown in the candlelight. Most of all, it was the pale white flesh, made even paler by the startling contrast of the dark lingerie encircling her waist, and encasing her lovely legs.

"You're beautiful in black silk," Katrina cooed. "You're beautiful in anything or nothing at all."

Katrina still harbored some suspicions that Svetlana would not be entirely willing to be the subservient provider of pleasure, which was now her role—whether she wanted it to be or not. But these suspicions were proven groundless when Svetlana crawled onto the bed. Katrina reached for her, thinking that Svetlana would need some of the soulful French kisses that Katrina had used so artfully before to strip away Svetlana's inhibitions. Instead, as Svetlana was crawling up the enormous mattress toward Katrina, she kissed the inside of Katrina's upraised knee. Slowly and sensually, Svetlana began nibbling up Katrina's leg. She started at the knee and moved up to the thigh. When she reached the special area where the thighs joined the pelvis, Svetlana did not hesitate. She kissed Katrina intimately, easing her tongue deeply between her-enflamed pussy lips.

This time it was Katrina Luvesky's turn to issue a startled cry. She looked down through the valley of her own breasts and could hardly believe that she was actually looking at the beautiful — and formerly reluctant — Svetlana Simonov, licking her cunt. The woman's nose was buried in the short, curly hair that grew above Katrina's pussy. Katrina could feel each subtle movement of Svetlana's tongue, each thrust, each parry, each swipe against her clit.

Katrina spread her arms out wide and cooed, "Come, my darlings. Show me that you love me!"

Vlad and Juanita soon were on the gigantic bed, nursing upon Katrina's breasts as Svetlana, lower on the mattress, continued performing the service that was expected of her.

CHAPTER TWELVE

A lberto Sacci looked at his Number One bodyguard, Bruno, and said, "Keep your eyes open. There's something about this dame that just ain't sittin' right with me. She ain't putting all her cards on the table, and I'd like to know why."

Bruno Furman studied his boss carefully. He had learned that some men have a sixth sense, and he believed that Sacci had a sixth, seventh, and eighth sense. That was why the Federal Bureau of Investigations had never been able to pin anything on him in all these years. That was why the Central Intelligence Agency had never been able to prove that he had ever done anything outside the borders of the United States except sightseeing. Bruno figured that hitching his wagon to Alberto Sacci was money in the bank.

"You figure she's settin' you up, boss?"

"Naw. I don't know what she ain't showin', but there's somethin'. My guts are tellin' me that, and I've been around long enough to listen to my guts." Sacci lit a cigar and savored the smoke for a moment. "Don't do nothing until I tell you," he continued. "But get your men ready. Most likely, it ain't nothin' at all. All I'm doing is reading the lady's fear, and thinkin' that fear is treachery. But if it ain't — if she's really trying to pull some kinda fast one — then I want you and the boys ready to rumble. You hearin' me?"

"Loud and clear, boss. Loud and clear."

"Good. Now get outta here. I got thinking to do. We're pickin' up the next shipment tomorrow night, and I want to

146

see in my head how everything is going to work."

"Sure, boss. Sure," the bodyguard said as he left the room. He could hardly imagine the brainpower it must take to envision an event that had not yet happened. The very notion that anyone might be capable of imagining such a thing seemed, to the gun-toting bodyguard, to be an act of almost superhuman intelligence.

As Svetlana stared at Katrina, she finally figured out what the other woman liked best. *It's all about power. What turns her on isn't the sex, and it isn't the drugs — it is being able to make people do things they don't want to do, and forcing them to smile the entire time they do it.*

She had learned a lot in the ninety minutes that she'd been in the *fun house,* as Katrina called the specially outfitted bedroom. Svetlana had learned that people were allowed to kiss, but only so long as Katrina told them to. Otherwise, no kissing. No caressing, either. If Katrina wanted to watch Juanita caressing Svetlana's breasts, she gave the command, and the action was immediately taken. But under no circumstances was Juanita to kiss Svetlana's breasts without being told to do so. As far as the drugs were concerned, they were all for Katrina. She was the only one smoking marijuana, snorting cocaine, drinking champagne, or taking Ecstasy. Everything — every last little nuance of the orgy — was focused upon Katrina Luvesky's whims, wishes, desires, and fetishes. In this room, she was an all-powerful goddess.

The room smelled of perfume, perspiration, and passion. Svetlana could hear the sound of moist flesh striking moist flesh. Only vaguely was she conscious of Vlad being on his knees behind Juanita, plowing into her with machine-like intensity. Juanita was busy using her lips on Katrina, who lay back with her legs spread obscenely wide apart. Svetlana was busy either kissing Katrina on the mouth — Katrina loved

French kisses, she explained, but only provided the kisser knew how to use her tongue properly—or sucking on Katrina's breasts. Katrina, it seemed, did not have orgasms easily, though she craved them with the desperation of a madwoman.

With a mixture of sorrow and sadistic delight, Svetlana realized that the drugs Katrina enjoyed aroused her but prevented her from having orgasms.

In the time she'd spent with Katrina, she had learned that the woman was the worst kind of human monster—the kind that didn't really see itself as a monster. Rather, Katrina viewed herself as a leader with a few minor quirks that should be ignored by her underlings. It would never occur to her that anyone would consider her a sadistic killer—even though one of her favorite delights was to watch Vlad the Impaler grab a man by the head and crush his skull between his palms.

Svetlana was sucking on Katrina's nipple, using her lips and tongue on the erect bud of flesh, when Katrina finally cried out in ecstasy. Almost immediately, Katrina pushed Svetlana away and lashed out with her bare feet, kicking at Juanita.

"Go . . .go away now," Katrina gasped, rolling onto her side as though her nudity suddenly embarrassed her.

Svetlana pulled her knees beneath her on the bed. Without warning, Vlad grabbed a handful of Svetlana's hair and pulled her backward off the bed. Svetlana had the good sense to not scream out in pain, though she had caught the giant's wrist to keep him from pulling too hard on her tresses. He pulled her off the bed, and it wasn't until she was outside in the hallway and the *fun house* door was closed that Vlad the Impaler at last released his hold on Svetlana's hair.

Juanita followed close behind.

"Once she's had her orgasm, she can't stand the sight of anyone," Juanita explained. The girl stood there in the hallway, her petite body glistening with perspiration. She was completely naked, though she seemed to pay this state of undress no mind at all. "Go to your room now. If you're needed further, I'll let you know."

"But my clothes are still in the room," Svetlana protested quietly. She held one hand down low to cover her femininity. Her other hand was crossed over her breasts in a futile attempt to hide them.

"Leave them. If you go back into the room, Comrade Luvesky will tell Vlad to crush your skull, and he will do exactly that without delay. Do not doubt me, American bitch. I mean every word I say."

Svetlana turned away from the unlikely duo of Juanita and Vlad, one a diminutive killer, the other a hulkish one. They frightened Svetlana to the core of her soul because she knew that they were capable of any barbarism imaginable.

When Svetlana reached her bedroom, she took a long, excruciatingly hot shower, washing her body with soap over and over again.

Memories of Vlad's enormous cock entering her, filling her, came to mind, and she forced the thoughts away. What she had done was for her country. She had been an actress, playing a role that had nothing to do with the person that she truly was. By the time she curled up in bed alone, she was able to remind herself that though Vlad had touched her body, he had not touched her soul.

Knowing that her soul was still untarnished by the night's activities, Svetlana closed her eyes and slept peacefully.

The following evening, Bruno Furman was sitting behind the wheel of a three-year-old Cadillac coupe. In the trunk was a suitcase filled with used American currency. Beneath his left arm, hidden by the fine tailoring of his suit coat, was a Taurus

9 mm. automatic. In the inside breast pocket of the jacket was a simple white envelope containing ten thousand dollars in cash.

"This ain't your pay," Alberto Sacci had said as he tucked the envelope into Bruno's pocket. "This is just a tip. You know, a little something extra just to say thanks for doin' a good job."

"Thanks, boss," Bruno replied.

"Now you keep your eyes open, right? Don't you let nobody get the jump on you. What you got in the trunk's a lot of dough, and I want something special in return for that dough."

Bruno opened his jacket enough to show the pistol in the clamshell shoulder holster. He gave his employer a cocky grin and explained, "They try anything funny, they ain't going to be laughing for long. You can count on me, boss."

"I'm doing exactly that, so don't you let me down," the Mafia kingpin said as he turned his back and started walking away. "I'll be seein' you later. You know what to do."

"Sure thing, boss. I know everything."

Bruno turned the key and the Cadillac's big V-8 engine came to life. A smile touched Bruno's mouth. Alberto Sacci had voiced his suspicions about the exchange tonight, and in the very same breath said that he trusted Bruno more than any of his other soldiers. If Bruno pulled off the switch and came back with a car carrying ninety-eight percent pure cocaine in the trunk, it would be his ticket to the big time. Sacci would trust him more and more all the time, and then, instead of being just a simple button man, he'd be a lieutenant, or maybe even a counselor and sit at the Sacci's right hand during negotiations.

The future was all laid out for Bruno, and all he had to do to see that his future was rosy was make sure that he exchanged a Cadillac filled with money for a Lincoln filled with narcotics.

He glanced at his wristwatch. It was seven minutes to midnight. Bruno figured he was three minutes from the meeting place — another seafood joint near the waterfront — so he slowed the Cadillac down a little. No sense in getting there early. That might draw attention. Attention was the last thing any Mafia soldier wanted.

He turned left near the pier, went around the block once, then did it a second time, just to make sure he wasn't being tailed. Confident he wasn't, Bruno pulled into the parking lot of Sunny Jo's Seaside Restaurant. The parking lot was crowded, and the place was hopping, just as it always was on a Friday night. Bruno pulled the Cadillac into a parking lot near the rear, turned off the engine and pocketed the keys, then got out of the car. He lit a cigarette and leaned back against the driver's side door. He looked like just another guy whose wife was taking too long in the bathroom before they made the drive home. People who entered the parking lot never gave him a second glance.

Bruno spotted the curvaceous, blonde-haired woman in the Lincoln the instant she turned into the parking lot. As the Lincoln crept slowly by, Bruno got a glance inside the car. Not even the poor lighting of the parking lot could disguise the extraordinary body the courier possessed.

"Holy Mother Mary," Bruno murmured beneath his breath, then felt guilty for speaking the name of the Mother Mary when such unholy thoughts were in his heart.

He watched as she found a parking spot just three down from his own. When she got out of the car, he was given a glimpse of thigh. She wore a dark blue knee-length skirt, with a matching blouse, a black belt, and high-heeled pumps. She didn't show a lot of skin, but she didn't need to in order to look sexy. It rather surprised Bruno that the blonde was being used as the go-between. It usually wasn't good form to pick anyone who would, by the nature of their appearance, draw attention. That was the reason that Sacci had been so surprised to see the Russian giant escorting Katrina Luvesky to the first meeting.

"Hi, stranger," the woman said as she sauntered forward. She was smiling with her lips, but Bruno could see the smile never reached her eyes. "You look like a man who's waiting for someone."

"Could be."

"I'm willing to bet you're waiting for me. I'm Svetlana. Katrina sent me."

Bruno let his gaze go up and down slowly. He couldn't guess her age with any degree of accuracy, and he was curious as hell as to whether her magnificent breasts were the result of God's blessings, or a plastic surgeon's skill. When his gaze finally came back up to her face, he smiled and nodded.

"I'm Bruno Furman. My boss sent me."

"What's the name of your boss? Maybe I know him."

"Sonny."

"Sonny? You call Alberto Sacci just plain *Sonny* and he'll cut your tongue out."

Bruno relaxed. That was the password. When he looked at Svetlana again, he wondered whether she might be willing to go out for a drink sometime. They couldn't do it right after the exchange, of course. He had to drive the Lincoln with all that cocaine back to Alberto Sacci. And she—well, she had to drive the Cadillac wherever she had been told to drive it. But maybe later, when neither of them were working, they might get together for a drink.

"Hey, I said it right, didn't I?"

Svetlana's words pulled Bruno out of his own thoughts. He flicked his cigarette away, and for the first time since getting out of his car, allowed his right hand to move more than just a few inches away from the butt of the Taurus in its clamshell holster.

"Just as right as rain," he said, already reaching into his pocket for the keys to the Cadillac.

They exchanged the keys, then inspected the trunks of each other's car. Neither of them moved quickly. Outwardly, they appeared to be just restaurant customers looking in the trunk for something they might have forgotten, were putting something in the trunk for safe keeping while in the restaurant.

When they returned to a point midway between the Cadillac and the Lincoln, Bruno said, "Let's take a walk, hold hands, and talk softly to each other."

They hardly walked thirty feet before stopping. When they turned to face each other, Bruno tried to ease his arms around Svetlana's slender waist, as though they were lovers. She gently but firmly declined the ruse.

"Hey, maybe sometime you and I could go out for a drink, or a bite to eat, huh?"

Svetlana looked at Bruno appraisingly, then slowly nodded and answered, "Sure. Sometime. But not when we're working. And not in Key West. I don't know if my boss would like me dating one of Alberto Sacci's soldiers."

"What she don't know won't hurt her."

Svetlana laughed and turned away, heading for the Cadillac. "I'll see you later, sport."

Bruno watched the sway of Svetlana's backside as she walked away. He had spent less than ten minutes in her company, but already he was entranced for life. He just knew it.

With a smile on his lips and a spring in his step, he jumped into the Lincoln, adjusted the seat and the rearview mirrors, then put the car in gear and pulled out of the parking lot. His thoughts were on Svetlana, but he forced himself to pay attention to his surroundings. This wasn't the time to get stopped by the cops. After all, he had a fortune in virtually pure cocaine in the trunk, and it would be real hard to pretend he didn't know it was there.

He kept an eye in his rearview mirror. Bruno liked to think that he could spot a tail even before it started. It wasn't unusual for him to spend as much time looking in the rearview mirrors as out the windshield.

What was surprising was that he suddenly saw thick, black smoke billowing out of his own trunk.

He slammed on the brakes, shut off the engine, and pulled the keys out of the ignition. Fifteen seconds later, despite the heat emanating from inside the trunk, he pulled open the trunk lid. Flames ten feet high rolled out of the trunk. Somewhere deep within all that fire was the cocaine that Bruno himself had inspected for purity.

Now it was all going up in flames.

Bruno took a dozen steps backward. It was the hottest fire he'd ever encountered in his life. Amazingly hot.

And right over the gasoline tank of the automobile.

Bruno ducked behind a parked car just in time. The Lincoln's gas tank exploded, sending the luxury sedan flipping through the air and shattering home windows for a hundred yards around.

Bruno had been given explicit instructions to never use the cellular telephone to call Alberto Sacci unless it was an absolute emergency. If this didn't qualify as an emergency, then nothing did. He thumbed the numbers into the telephone as he walked away from the burning wreck of the Lincoln. Millions of dollars' worth of pure cocaine was going up in smoke, and there wasn't a damn thing that Bruno could do about it.

"Yeah?"

"Boss, it's me. Listen, something happened."

"What? And be careful. We got a lotta ears listening in on these cordless things."

"Yeah. I know. But listen . . .I don't know how to tell you, but there was a fire in the trunk. A real bad fire. I can't tell you why it started, it just did. Before I knew it, the whole car was in flames."

Dead silence followed. Bruno felt sweat running down his face. He felt sick in his soul like he'd never felt before.

"Boss, are you still there?"

"Yeah, I'm still here. Listen, you got set up. I felt it in my gut all along. You got set up from jump street. You get back here right away."

"Sure, boss."

"You get back here. She thinks she's safe behind that big wall she's got, but she don't know squat."

"Sure thing, boss."

"I'm getting a crew together, and we're getting our money back. You hear what I'm saying?"

"Sure, boss. Sure. And listen, I'm real sorry about—"

Bruno stopped talking when the line went dead. All Bruno could think about was whether Alberto Sacci would kill him, and whether the gorgeous woman named Svetlana had set him up.

He started looking for a taxi cab. He had to get to a walled-in mansion complex at the end of the island. There was a war to be fought, and if he was to redeem himself in Sacci's eyes, then he had to find that redemption on the field of battle.

He had to get Alberto Sacci his millions back, or he'd be dead. The Mafia don was giving him one last chance.

It was just as simple as that.

While driving the sedan, Svetlana Simonov looked at the remote control in her right hand.

How the hell does Omega Force get me everything I need so quickly? There must be a gazillion people working behind the scenes.

The oblong black instrument was similar in appearance to a remote control for a television, but its purpose wasn't nearly so innocuous. When she touched her thumb to the center button, a small green light began to glow. The light glowed for three seconds, blinked on and off for another ten, then went off for good.

Svetlana smiled. There was now a blazing fire that would burn at an extraordinary temperature in the trunk of the sedan. There was absolutely no doubt in Svetlana's mind that within five minutes, there wouldn't be a single milligram of salvageable cocaine left.

Alberto Sacci's going to go ballistic when he finds out his cocaine's nothing but smoke.

It was a comforting thought for Svetlana. She had accepted a mission to find out whether Sir Malcomb Sitwell had actually killed his family and then committed suicide, or whether foul play had put an end to the retired intelligence officer's life. Svetlana was now certain that Sir Malcomb had been murdered, and that Katrina Luvesky had ordered the murder. Who exactly pulled the trigger, she did not know. She actually wasn't very curious to know. The actual murderers were secondary — the real crime rested on the soul of the person who ordered the murders.

It had been sheer coincidence that Svetlana had been put in a position where she could damage the Moscow Cartel's American drug operation, but once she saw she had the opportunity, she knew she had to make the most of her chance. As she drove back to headquarters, she wondered how furious Alberto Sacci would be when he learned the high-grade cocaine he had just purchased was now low-grade air pollution.

Svetlana wondered what Sacci's first response would be. Attack? Possibly. More likely he'd take the time to get his forces set up, then demand that Katrina give his money back. It wouldn't be until Katrina refused to refund the money — the money which, at that very moment, was in the trunk of the car Svetlana was driving — that the shooting would start.

As she drove, Svetlana thought about what her own next

moves would be. Though she had just now damaged a major drug running operation, there was still the issue of Katrina Luvesky's guilt that had not been addressed . . .

CHAPTER THIRTEEN

K atrina was nervous, though she wasn't letting it show. Svetlana wasn't late. Yet. She wasn't due back for another fifteen minutes, but Katrina's stomach was knotted with tension anyway. She hadn't sent anyone to follow Svetlana to guarantee that the suitcase full of money made it from the exchange site back to headquarters. Katrina was beginning to think that maybe she should have sent Juanita or Rutgar to follow Svetlana — just to be on the safe side.

There would have been nothing safe about doing that at all! The agreement with Sacci was that when the full shipments began, there wouldn't be any extra muscle along. Svetlana will come back. She knows how to follow orders. She does . . .I'm sure she does . . .

But no matter how hard Katrina tried to convince herself that everything was going according to plan, she couldn't entirely silence the small but insistent voice of suspicion that haunted her.

The library door opened and Juanita stepped in.

Katrina's face was pale but her voice was steady as she asked, "What is it?"

"She's here, Comrade Luvesky."

A smile exploded on Katrina's face.

"Just like I planned!" Katrina exclaimed as she burst out of her overstuffed chair.

Juanita pushed the door open wide and stepped out of the way as Katrina hurried past her, taking long strides.

Alberto Sacci looked at the shotgun in his hands. At the corners of his mouth was the hint of a smile. The shotgun was a double-barrel twelve gauge, with the barrels cut off at the end of the forearm stock. The pockets of his expensively tailored suit coat were bulging with shells for the weapon.

How long had it been since he'd actually participated in any of the nitty-gritty strong-arm tactics that were so often necessary in the Mafia? He couldn't remember with certainty the last time he had willingly put himself into a position where he might get caught in crossfire.

There was the time three years earlier, when he'd caught one of his bookkeepers skimming money, but that didn't really count. Sacci had taken effective measures to see that the skimming ended. He'd walked up to the bookkeeper as he was sitting at his desk, then shot the man in the back of the head, blowing his brains all over the computer. But that wasn't the same as willingly going into what was sure to be a hot gunfight.

Sacci was in the back seat of a Lincoln. He had all his best men in the car with him, the men he knew he could count on to not run for the tall grass when the shooting started. Bruno Furman was driving. When the men discovered that their leader himself was going along on the raid at the compound, every single one of them looked at Sacci as though seeing him in a whole new and very flattering, light. This was an act of courage they hadn't anticipated. Alberto Sacci was a man who gave orders to soldiers, but he didn't behave like a foot soldier himself. Not until tonight.

More than he had in months, Alberto Sacci felt like a leader of men.

"I don't know how they fooled Bruno, but they fooled him," Sacci said as he thumbed two shells into the shotgun. He snapped the weapon closed with authority. "That Russian bitch didn't burn up millions of dollars' worth of cocaine. She burned up just enough to make us think she did. She took the money and she didn't come across with the cocaine. Tonight we're getting the money back. Tonight we're getting our dignity back, because we're Americans and we ain't getting conned by no stinkin' Russian!"

"That's right, boss. That's right!" Bruno said, his voice rising as he sped past much slower moving cars.

"Damn right, that's right!" the button man in the front passenger seat said as he slapped a thirty-round staggered-row magazine into the butt of an Uzi submachine gun. "We're getting it all back tonight!"

Katrina finished counting the money. Millions of dollars in American currency, all in hundred-dollar bills. The built-in wall safe the mansion's original owners had installed was not terribly large. It was already stuffed with money from Sacci's original down payment for the drug running operation. There wasn't room for the additional cash.

It was a nice problem to have. Katrina pushed herself off her bed, closed the lid of the enormous wheeled suitcase filled with money, then went to the wall safe and closed it, too. She gave the dial a spin. She tucked the suitcase beneath her king-sized bed and left her bedroom. She wanted to inspect the mini submarine. That was the key to the operation. Cocaine from South America, purified in Cuba, then dropped to the ocean floor just beyond the United States's recognized territorial waters. The DEA could search until they were blue in the face and they'd never figure out how the Moscow Cartel was thwarting their best efforts at drug interdiction.

She stepped out of her bedroom and nearly bumped into Juanita.

"I'm going to check out the sub," Katrina said quietly, her gaze soft and warm, like they usually were after a very successful operation. "Want to come with?"

"Yes, Comrade Luvesky."

Katrina could hear Rutgar playing billiards with some of his men in a room on the main floor. The men were laughing. Katrina had already personally inspected the guards Rutgar had posted, so she wasn't concerned with security. Rutgar was a professional through and through, though a bit prone to resorting to unnecessary violence. It was this trigger-happy aspect to the man that had previously caused Katrina to keep him at arm's length.

"The new men — you approve of them?" Juanita asked as she opened the mansion's southern door for Katrina.

"Yes, but with some reservations." Katrina stepped outside. It was a cloudy night, and the stars could not be seen. She could see two of Rutgar's men at the stone wall, each one carrying a pump-action shotgun. "Any ideas on who attacked us the other night?" Katrina asked. "No matter how I look at the situation, I can't make sense of it."

It wasn't often that Katrina asked her opinion on anything, certainly not on anything as important as the attack on the headquarters. Juanita was visibly flattered, and it showed in the brightness in her eyes. "No, Comrade Luvesky, I do not. But maybe Mr. Bigg will have some ideas. He seems to know everything."

"You're right, of course. Mr. Bigg will figure it out."

They reached the submarine's boathouse. Katrina gave a nod to the soldier standing guard, and he stepped aside. When she was inside the boathouse, she turned on the overhead lights. The mini submarine gleamed in the light, its exterior shiny and clean, its lines smooth to cut effortlessly through the water.

"We're going to make a lot of money for Mr. Bigg with this submarine," Katrina said. She touched the exterior of the vessel in a caressing manner. "More kilograms of nearly pure cocaine every week . . . think of the profits, Juanita. Just think of the profits."

The sound of submachine gun fire drowned out Juanita's reply.

Svetlana was standing barefooted in her bedroom, wearing just her brassiere and panties. She felt tired to the bone. The tension of living inside what was, in effect, the enemy's camp was taking its toll on her nerves. She wanted to kick back in a luxury hotel room in Washington D.C., or some other capital in the world, with her feet up, wearing an old flannel night-gown or perhaps nothing at all. She wanted to watch a few Cary Grant movies. But that would have to wait. First she had to dish up some justice to a murderous Russian woman with eyes as cold as ice.

She was just reaching to unhook the brassiere's closures be-tween her shoulder blades when a chugging burst of auto-matic weapon fire ripped through the silence of the night. Svetlana was sitting at the edge of her bed. For a split second in time she looked at her own reflection in the mirror.

Was Alberto Sacci making his move already?

A glimmer of a smile touched her lips. Could she possibly have started an all-out gunfight between the Moscow Cartel and Alberto Sacci's branch of the Mafia? That was almost too good to hope for.

The unmistakably thunderous roar of a twelve-gauge shot-gun put an end to any uncertainties for Svetlana. She was now in the middle of a gunfight between two armies, both of whom she opposed. Each death, either to Sacci and his men, or to the Moscow Cartel, was a victory for Svetlana and for freedom.

Her first move was to hurry to her suitcase. Another burst of machine gun fire ripped through the night. Svetlana's movements were swift and sure as she opened the hidden compartment in the base to reveal two pistols, along with a titanium silencer. She didn't have much time. Taking the HSc, she pinched the Mauser's magazine release to extract the clip that held the Sleeping Beauties. For what was happening now, she needed semi-jacketed hollow-point ammunition. She slapped in a fresh seven-shot magazine, drew the slide back to charge the weapon, then attached the titanium silencer to the Mauser's muzzle. Lastly, she plucked out two additional magazines and, holding them in her left hand, hurried out her bedroom door.

It had been less than a minute since the first eruption of machine gun fire had cut through the night, but already the chaos going on downstairs was considerable. Soldiers were getting out of bed. Others were hurrying to where their weapons were stashed. Outside, the booming reports from shotguns now answered those of the bursts of machine gun fire. The war, it seemed to Svetlana, was being conducted on at least three of the four sides of the estate.

The last Svetlana had seen of Katrina, she was headed for her bedroom and carrying the suitcase that had been in the Lincoln's trunk. Svetlana ran barefooted down the hall, her heavy breasts bouncing inside the lacy brassiere. She had just reached Katrina's bedroom door when, from the near end of the hallway, a soldier hurried up the stairs and rounded the corner. He was carrying a slide-action shotgun and, like Svetlana, was wearing only his underwear. He looked at Svetlana and his eyes widened in shock; then he noticed the pistol with the silencer in her hand. He swung the shotgun around.

Svetlana's reactions were faster. She squeezed the trigger, and the Mauser jumped in her hand, hissing a sigh of death. The .32-caliber hollow-point punched into the German's stomach just beneath the sternum. The soldier staggered a step backward and reflexively squeezed the trigger of the shotgun. Buckshot ripped into the wall to the right of Svetlana. She fired a second time. A neat, round hole formed in the soldier's naked chest directly over his heart. Blood fountained out like water from a hose. The gunman tumbled backward down the stairs he had just climbed, the shotgun clattering loudly against the marble steps.

Svetlana opened Katrina's door and stepped inside. The Mauser in her right hand searched for the bedroom's occupant. Katrina had to pay for her crime against Sir Malcomb Sitwell and his family, and there was no better time to see that she pay the ultimate price than right now, when one more death amidst the carnage of a gangland war would be nothing more than an additional paragraph in the morning newspapers.

But the bedroom was empty.

Svetlana stepped deeper into the room, her sea-blue eyes darting here and there, the Mauser tracking with her gaze for a target that would not materialize.

From the hallway stairs came heard a startled shout. Svetlana's first victim had been found. She turned, aiming at the open doorway. The second man to show himself would end up as dead as the first. That was Svetlana's plan — right up to the time she heard what sounded like at least four or five pairs of boots pounding against the stairs as they hurried to the second floor of the mansion. Svetlana didn't like the odds.

The bedroom was very large, and the walk-in closet was the perfect place to hide. Only it was all the way across the room and it would force Svetlana to run closer to the door instead of away from it. Taking the only avenue of concealment left to her, she tossed herself to the floor, using the bed to hide herself from the doorway. Not two seconds had passed before she heard men at the doorway.

"See anybody?"

Katrina's bed was a large four-poster affair, and it was just high enough for Svetlana to wriggle silently under. Her heart was pounding. She did her best to keep her breathing as quiet as possible as Rutgar's men cautiously entered the room. They fanned out, moving like professional fighting men. If Svetlana was spotted, the end would be instantaneous and savage. Outside, sporadic machine gun fire mingled with the booming reports of shotguns, and the occasional crack of a pistol.

"Room's empty," one of the soldiers said, his English thick with a German accent. "Let's keep moving."

Another voice added, also in English though his accent was Norwegian, "Mr. Bigg will have our skin taken off in strips if we let anything happen to his lady!"

Boots thudded against the floor as the men hurried out of the bedroom in search of Katrina Luvesky.

Still beneath the bed, Svetlana closed her eyes for a moment and breathed a sigh of relief. She wanted to take *more* than just a moment to calm her nerves and compose herself, but she didn't have the time, and she knew it. She began wriggling out from her hiding spot . . .and that's when she realized she wasn't alone beneath the bed. There was a familiar piece of luggage with her.

Svetlana pulled the suitcase out, sliding it over the carpet. She had earlier carried it from the trunk of the luxury sedan into the mansion. Now, with her left hand, she flicked open the locks, glanced at the bedroom door to assure herself that she was still alone, then opened the lid. It was all there. Millions of American dollars in used hundreds. Benjamin Franklin had never looked so handsome.

A burst of laughter escape Svetlana's throat, despite the escalating gunfire outside the mansion. Not much earlier, she had put in motion a fire which burned up an enormous brick of virtually pure cocaine. Now, completely by accident, she was in possession of millions of dollars in Mafia cash. The irony of it all was delicious.

"Karmic justice," Svetlana murmured as she snapped closed the lid of the suitcase.

With nowhere else to put the extra ammunition for her seven-shot Mauser, Svetlana tucked the magazines in her brassiere between her breasts, then lifted the suitcase in her left hand. Her old-fashioned Mauser, so scorned by her lover and leader, Jefferson Burke, was still in her right hand, steady and reliable as always.

Svetlana was at the bedroom door when a trailing soldier in Rutgar's command turned the corner and found himself face-to-face with an incredibly buxom, incredibly beautiful blonde woman wearing only bikini panties and a brassiere. He died with two quick, silent rounds of .32-caliber hollow-point ammunition going through his heart. Death came so quickly, he never knew what hit him.

Katrina looked out the boathouse door. The firefight was in full swing. Rutgar's men, all seasoned professionals, were fighting gamely against an opposing force that was well-armed, numerous, but less seasoned. Despite their undisciplined, unschooled approach to warfare, it was clear to the Katrina that her forces would soon be completely overrun.

Katrina shouted to the two mercenaries standing near the boathouse, "Join the attack, you fools!"

The soldiers rushed off to join the fray.

Inside Katrina's brain, a question screamed insistently. Why would Alberto Sacci do this? Why attack, when he had so much to gain by going into business? The question had no answer that Katrina could comprehend.

"Comrade Luvesky, do you want me to stay with you, or join the attack?"

Katrina looked down at the slender girl beside her. "Stay

with me," she said after a moment, pleased, as always, with Juanita's loyalty. "Prepare the submarine for immediate departure."

Without a word, Juanita hurried over to the computerized control panel against the wall of the boathouse. She pushed a toggle switch forward. Lights on the panel flickered briefly, then glowed solid green.

Katrina again looked out the door. She watched as a man wearing a tailored business suit rushed toward one of Rutgar's men, shooting a pump-action shotgun from the hip. The soldier, carrying a submachine gun, opened up on his assailant. Katrina was shocked at the violence of the moment as blood spurted from both men simultaneously, misting the air pink in the dim light. The mercenary and the mobster both crumpled to the ground, writhing briefly before making a final death-twitch in the grass.

Katrina turned toward the mini submarine. She hopped onto it, grabbing the top hatch handle and giving it a hard twist.

"Hurry, Juanita," the lanky blonde commanded. "At least you and I will get away from here alive."

"To fight another day, Comrade Luvesky?"

Katrina opened the hatch door and slipped into the mini submarine.

Alberto Sacci liked the way the battle was going. His guys were going to win. Perfect. His men were inside the mansion, mopping up the last of the resistance and searching for millions of dollars in cash. They'd find it soon, Sacci knew. The soldier who found the money would be given at least a hundred thousand dollars in cash, and that was the kind of incentive that made a killer out of every man he'd ever hired.

With the outcome now secure, Sacci decided it was time for

him to guarantee his own survival. Rushing into battle because he'd been ripped off by a Russian bitch was a move that had guaranteed the respect and obedience of his men. It was time now, though, to get serious and think about the future.

A fire had started inside the mansion, and three-foot flames of blue and orange were licking out of one upstairs window. Two windows away, on the same floor, a gunman smashed out the glass, stuck his head of the opening, and shouted, "I found the safe! I found the safe!"

Sacci watched as three of his men hurried toward the mansion.

Yes, that's right, boys. Dig the safe out of the wall if you have to. Sacci was already calculating what kind of bonuses he was going to give to his men for this operation.

He turned away from the burning mansion and slipped out through the front gates. His Lincoln was parked thirty yards from the entrance. As he walked toward his vehicle, the double-barrel shotgun in his hands, there was a swagger to his stride—a lightness of step that hadn't been there in years.

He was nearly to his luxury sedan when movement to his left caught his attention. Sacci turned, raising the barrels of the shotgun, holding the weapon at his hip. A smile touched his lips when he saw the stunning blonde. She wore matching brassiere and panties, and looked every bit as erotically enticing as she ever had. Better still, in her left hand was the suitcase that, unless Sacci was very much mistaken, was the one he'd used to transport millions in cash.

"Isn't this a nice surprise?" Sacci aimed the shotgun at the woman's naked stomach. "I see you've brought me a present."

Svetlana stood motionless, her breasts rising and falling with her rapid breathing. The suitcase was in her left hand at her side, and her right hand was behind her back.

"Let's see your hands." Sacci raised the aim of his shotgun to the woman's breasts. "Real easy. I can cut you in half with this thing."

Svetlana's right hand went down to her side. The Mauser with its sausage-like silencer surprised Sacci. It was a professional's weapon. One that would have been perfect in his hand. What would a dolly like Svetlana be doing with a silenced automatic? Alberto Sacci had always had a difficult time taking women seriously.

"Drop the gun and suitcase, then get on your knees."

"Taking off before the battle's over? Little cowardly, isn't it?"

"Don't mess with me! There's not another wiseguy in the whole country with the stones to do what I've just done!" Sacci showed his teeth. It was more of a canine snarl than a smile. "Better still, get over to the Lincoln. You and the money go into the trunk. I'll figure out what to do with you later."

She walked to the rear of the Lincoln.

"I told you to drop the gun. Don't think I won't shoot a woman."

At the trunk, the woman turned to face Sacci.

He swept his gaze slowly up and down over the statuesque body of the blonde. He made no effort to hide his lust. "Last warning. Drop the gun or I'll blow you away."

"Are you really that fast?"

"Fast? Honey, all I've got to do is squeeze the trigger."

She dropped the suitcase. It landed heavily on the ground at her bare feet.

Sacci's eyes flicked from Svetlana's face to the suitcase. It was a fatal mistake. The instant Sacci looked at the suitcase, Svetlana tilted the Mauser and caressed the trigger. The pistol jumped in her hand, issuing a coughing sound. A single, round hole formed in Sacci's chest. A look of confusion registered in his eyes. He looked down and watched as a red stain spread across the starched white surface of his dress shirt. He turned his attention back to Svetlana. She was standing with her feet spread, holding the Mauser in both hands now. *She's shot me! The rotten bitch shot me!*

The double-barrel shotgun suddenly weighed a hundred pounds. A moment later it weighed two hundred. Sacci tried to keep the barrels aimed at the woman's stomach, but the shotgun just kept getting heavier and heavier. He squeezed the trigger and the weapon roared. Dirt and grass kicked up at his feet. The shotgun's recoil was too powerful for Sacci, and the weapon fell to the ground.

Alberto Sacci fell to his knees. Sacci heard her say, "I've always liked Detroit luxury cars. Are the keys in the ignition?"

Sacci listened as the Lincoln drove away. A moment later he heard the wail of a police siren. Then he heard nothing at all.

EPILOGUE

Washington D.C.

"Nice job with the Sitwell mess," Burke said, looking at the field agent in his hotel room. It never failed to impress him how attractive she was, and how deadly and competent.

"Thank you," Svetlana Simonov replied. "Of course, Katrina Luvesky is still out there somewhere, so it wasn't a complete success."

The general smiled. "Yes, she's out there, but you've smashed her entire operation. The Moscow Cartel might still exist, but it isn't what it had been. Its power structure is in shambles, and since your assault on their American site, we've been able to track much of their financial operations. Before you got involved, we hadn't even heard of the Moscow Cartel—now we know the organization inside and out. Or so it seems. Pity that monstrous giant we've got in custody can't tell us anything. I guess he's known as *Vlad the Impaler.* Any idea why?"

Svetlana crossed her legs at the knee before adjusting the hem of her skirt. She shook her head. Svetlana could feel her lover watching her every move.

"You've been able to freeze their finances?" she asked.

"Freeze? Ha! We've confiscated most of it."

Svetlana's jaw dropped open. "You're kidding, aren't you?"

"Not even a little. So far we've taken nearly one hundred million dollars' worth of the Moscow Cartel's cash right out of the banks they were in. We'll be using that money to attack them at every turn."

"How did you get the banks to release the money?"

"I don't have to remind you that money laundering is illegal. Omega Force simply convinced certain key officers of each bank that had been laundering money for the Moscow Cartel that unless they cooperated fully and completely, we would consider those banking officers as co-conspirators in terrorism. That means that the next time the Moscow Cartel puts out a contract for the assassination of a rival, the banker becomes just as responsible."

Svetlana's smile broadened. "The bankers know they won't do time for money laundering, but getting hit with a charge of murder in the first degree looks a whole lot different to them."

"Precisely."

Svetlana cleared her throat and looked away for a moment. "What about the suitcase, sir? I've brought it up twice with you since the mission was over. You've never really given me an answer."

He smiled with good humor. "Now technically, legally, that money belongs to Alberto Sacci. As soon as Sacci comes to claim it, and can prove he earned it legally, you'll have to give it back. Of course, that'll be several decades after hell freezes over. Until that time, since it was never money that belonged to the government, I don't see why you shouldn't use it however you see fit."

"No questions asked, sir?"

"No questions asked."

Svetlana leaned back in her chair, contemplating what she could do with millions of dollars of discretionary income. It was a pleasant problem to consider.

After several seconds, Burke said, "However, there is something you should be aware of."

Svetlana leaned forward in her chair, her senses alert, the bonus she'd just receive completely forgotten.

"Yes, sir?"

"There's been some curious goings on in Puerto Rico that I find . . . well, let's just say that we'd like to have answers to questions that, so far, have eluded us." He touched a button on his computer. He sighed as though suddenly weary. "You'll be out there on your own, I'm afraid. Omega Force is changing. Too damned many politicians are speaking to the press, and the intelligence services now have distinctly divided loyalties. There are still fools out there who don't quite understand that we're in a war and have to fight it like warriors." He shrugged his broad shoulders as though to rid himself of the political thoughts. "I'm having the information uploaded to a disk as we speak. Is that *uploaded* or *downloaded?*"

Svetlana eyes were bright and alive as she answered, "I believe it's *downloaded.*"

The End

You may also enjoy the following from eXtasy Books Inc:

To Kill Again
Robin Gideon

Excerpt

"And how is my lady?" Colonel Mendoza asked as he slid into the booth to sandwich Svetlana between himself and Palmero.

"What took you so long?" Svetlana demanded, her brow furrowed, her full-lipped mouth turned downward slightly at the edges in annoyance. "I started to worry that you'd never come back."

"Not come back to you?" Mendoza exclaimed, leaning away from her in mock horror, a hand lifting theatrically to his chest. "How could you even think such a thing?"

Palmero noticed that Svetlana placed her right hand upon Mendoza's thigh, midway between his knee and groin. Now that Mendoza had returned, she no longer had her hand on his leg. As a man who played power politics every day of his life, he understood her actions and didn't begrudge them. He didn't necessarily like what she had done, but he certainly understood it. He was a player who knew how to play the game . . . and he played it exceptionally well.

She said petulantly, just loud enough for both men to hear, "It's happened before. I'm always afraid that it'll happen again." She sniffled. "You can't blame me for that."

Svetlana crossed her legs delicately at the knee. She was wearing a dark green knee-length silk dress, the bodice of which only partially hid the sweet fullness of her bosom. Completely hiding the woman's extraordinary breasts was an impossibility, but it was clear from the tailoring of the garment that she was doing what she could to de-emphasize her more than ample charms.

The smile was gone now from her lips, and when she picked up her cocktail — a gin and tonic — in unladylike fashion, she finished it in three quick swallows.

"You need another," Mendoza said. It was a statement, not a question, and he was already raising his arm to get the waitress' attention.

"Yes, I need another," Svetlana replied. "But darling, won't you please go get it yourself? The waitress here is so overworked it takes her forever to serve the drinks."

Palmero looked at Mendoza. It was obvious he didn't like the idea of leaving her again. Better to hurry off and return with more liquor than let her sober up. He didn't want her to reach the conclusion that maybe the smart move to make was to go back to her hotel alone instead of to his hotel.

The general could read his right-hand man as though his emotions were printed words in ink on a page. He could read all the men who worked for him like a book, and it was a skill that had served him well for many years.

The colonel slipped out of the booth and pushed himself forcefully through the mass of bodies, heading toward the bar.

As soon as she was alone again with the general, Svetlana twisted in the padded bench seat toward Palmero. Her smile was electric, and the glow in her shimmering blue eyes was intoxicating.

"You're staying at the First Imperial Hotel?" she asked.

Palmero nodded. "We've got most of the ninth floor."

"How far away is your room from Colonel Mendoza's?"

"Right next door."

Svetlana looked away from Palmero toward the crowd, as though frightened that Mendoza might return and somehow hear the conversation she was having, even though the recorded electronic dance music blaring from the innumerable speakers made such an event impossible.

"He's . . . a strong man," Svetlana explained in an almost apologetic tone. "But he's only the beta male. You're the alpha male, aren't you?"

Palmero frowned. He had a solid grasp of the English language, but he didn't have a clue as to what Svetlana was speaking of now. The fact that she spoke English with a Russian accent didn't help. When he let his confusion show in his expression, she quickly explained what she meant by alpha and beta. Only then did he let awareness show in his expression. When he looked down into Svetlana's cleavage, he didn't make any effort to hide the direction of his gaze. Her words were making his cock even harder.

"I don't want to leave Mendoza for you," Svetlana said. "Not . . . not just yet. Not like this. It wouldn't be fair to him."

Palmero wasn't inclined to gaze too deeply into his good fortune. He knew that many of his sexual conquests had wanted something from him. Quite often they were young female soldiers looking for an easy assignment in the military. Other times they were hoping to get a promotion, or a transfer to a better military outfit. But whatever it was, whenever a beautiful woman threw herself at him, it was because they wanted something. They were just using their bodies and his lust to get his good graces—and he didn't have a problem with that. For Palmero, sex was a commodity that was either bartered for, or simply bought and paid for. But whatever it was, it wasn't something that a woman gave away for free. Not ever.

"What do you suggest?" Palmero asked after several

seconds of silence. For one of the few times in his adult life, he felt out of his element, confused and disoriented. It wasn't a feeling that sat well with him. He liked being in control.

"Go back to your hotel. I'll meet you there."

Svetlana put her hand over Palmero's crotch. When she squeezed him, he felt her fingers against his cock through the fabric of his trousers. He began to respond instantly. His cock had been on high alert from the first moment he'd set eyes on her. But at first he hadn't thought it would be possible that she would toss the colonel overboard for him. Now he understood that such a possibility was very real. The awareness added fuel to the fire in his libido.

He had close-cropped, gray hair, and though he was clearly a man of advancing years, he felt terribly young and virile.

"I don't know how I'll do it," Svetlana said, her Russian-laced speech apparently slurred by alcohol, "but I'll meet you there. And Colonel Mendoza won't know anything about it."

Palmero's eyes widened as he felt Svetlana's slender fingers caressing him intimately. How long had it been since he'd had a beautiful woman touching his cock like that? He couldn't remember the last time any woman—ugly or gorgeous, it didn't matter—had put a hand between his legs without being coerced into doing it. Whoever the fuck this Svetlana was, she was turning him on like no woman had in years.

"You're teasing me now," Palmero said quietly. The words shocked him, because he hadn't thought of actually speaking them. Svetlana seemed so sophisticated, so unobtainable, that he couldn't entirely believe that she wasn't just toying with his emotions for some bizarre, sadistic reason that he did not yet understand. "You're not actually going to come to my room."

"Promise me you'll wait for me in your room?"

"Come with me now. I'm a general and he's just a colonel," Palmero explained. "I don't know how much you know about the military, but a general far outranks a colonel." He inhaled deeply, squared his shoulders, and said, "I can make the little son of a bitch do whatever the fuck I tell him to do."

Svetlana shook her head, then combed her fingers through her blonde hair. To Palmero, it seemed an incredibly erotic gesture to make, though there wasn't anything outwardly erotic about it. Everything Svetlana did seemed to arouse him sexually.

"I know enough to realize that I want you to fuck me, and that the power you have over everyone around you turns me on. How's that? But I don't want to make the colonel angry, don't you see? Mendoza brought me here. Please"—she squeezed his cock again, then reached deeper between his legs to give his testicles some tender attention—"go back to your hotel and wait there for me. I'll be there soon. I promise I will."

Palmero felt the firm, enticing fingers toying with him, and he just knew that no woman fondling him like that could be a liar. He cast a quick glance in the direction of the bar, worried that Mendoza would return too quickly. He said, "Give me something . . . just a little something to know that you'll be by later. Do that for me, and I'll wait for you until eternity freezes over."

Mendoza was pushing his way through the crowd, moving toward the booth in the back of the nightclub. He had a vodka martini in one hand and a gin and tonic in the other. Much of the vodka martini had been spilled, apparently as he was pushing his way through the crowd of men. He was protecting the gin and tonic—Svetlana's drink—like his life depended upon it. There could be no doubt that he was more interested in getting alcohol into Svetlana's blood steam than into his own.

Mendoza set the gin and tonic down in front of Svetlana, then slid into the booth. He gave Svetlana and Palmero a careful look. He didn't trust Palmero with women, and it was obvious. At least not with women that Mendoza was hoping to keep for himself. Palmero smiled, feeling quite superior.

"My good colonel!" Palmero said, smiling broadly. There was a theatrical quality to his expression. "This has been a fine evening, but I think it is time I leave you alone with this young lady. I've stayed in this noisy nightclub too long as it is." He pushed himself out of the booth, and raised a hand when Mendoza began to put up what was at best a half-hearted protest at his departure. "I've overstayed my welcome as it is. You two stay here." He leaned over the table so that his face was close to Mendoza's. "I'll leave the car and driver here for you and take a taxi back to the hotel."

Mendoza replied, in a hushed voice that Svetlana was not to hear, "I owe you one, sir. And I won't forget it."

Palmero nodded to Mendoza, then straightened, looked at Svetlana, and smiled appreciatively. "Perhaps we will meet again."

Svetlana replied, "Perhaps we shall." She smiled. Her gaze never left Palmero's. "I hope we do."

Palmero turned and walked through the crowd. Unlike with Mendoza, when Palmero walked, other men got out of the way.

ABOUT THE AUTHOR

Robin Gideon is the author of over 50 novels and novellas in paperback form and for e-publishers. She is currently writing erotic action-adventure stories starring the secret agent Svetlana Simonov exclusively for eXtasy Books. She was the featured author on the nationally syndicated TV series CBS Sunday Morning. She loves hearing from her readers, and can be reached at: robin.gideon@ymail.com.